PRAISE FOR *WE CAN'T HELP IT...*

WE CAN'T HELP IT IF WE'RE FROM FLORIDA

NEW STORIES FROM A SINKING PENINSULA

edited by Shane Hinton

BURROW PRESS | ORLANDO, FL

Published by Burrow Press
PO Box 533709
Orlando, FL 32853
burrowpress.com

Cover Art: BoyKong
Lizard Illustration: Alex Lenhoff
Book Design: Liesl Swogger & Tina Craig

First Edition Hardcover
ISBN: 978-1-941681-87-9
LCCN: 2016957443
eBook ISBN: 978-1-941681-88-6

Distributed by Itasca Books
orders@itascabooks.com

Burrow Press is supported in part by its subscribers and:

ACKNOWLEDGEMENTS

This anthology is named after the hardcore/punk record *We Can't Help It If We're From Florida*, a compilation of Florida-based bands and labels put out by Destroy Records in 1983. All the authors in this collection are either current or former Florida residents. Some who grew up here have since left the state, but visit frequently. Others have vowed to never come back. Many of us are still here, mostly by choice.

TABLE OF CONTENTS

WHAT IS FLORIDA LITERATURE?

SHANE HINTON

Somewhere in Florida there is a puddle of rainwater. It's out of the way—you wouldn't see it unless you went looking for it in drainage ditches and retention ponds, under oak trees and palmetto bushes. It is tepid and almost entirely undisturbed, refreshed every afternoon by summer thunderstorms so regular you can nearly tell the time of day by the cloud cover. The puddle is light green. In the still water, tadpoles swim in tight circles. Their tails flutter behind them. They collide with wiggling mosquito larvae. In just a few days one will eat the other, but for now they share the same space, birthed by the same water.

Down the street there is a young mother, pregnant with her second child, swatting at a mosquito on the back of her neck. Tomorrow the bite will be red and inflamed. She will wake up in the night to scratch it. A virus slips in her bloodstream between heartbeats. It spreads to her brain, to her unborn child. Her fever will be so low that she will not even go to the doctor. She will think herself cured before the week is out. A truck drives by trailing a chemical mist from sprayers installed in its bed, distributing poison that will kill the larval mosquitoes before they can break free of the water, but it is already too late.

A rattlesnake is coiled beneath the young mother's front porch, in the cold dirt, out of the sun. She steps over it on the way to pick up her daughter from daycare, a few weathered two-by-fours all that separates them. Later that afternoon, her daughter will walk up the same stairs. The snake will watch silently, knowing it can strike for more than half of its body length. The daughter has not yet learned this fact of Florida life. Her class is working on colors. Before he died, her grandfather taught her how to identify coral snakes. Red on yellow, kill a fellow, she remembers him saying, although the words have little meaning. She has never seen a coral snake.

The girl plays in the front room as the afternoon thunderstorm rolls in. Out the window she watches the branches of tall water oaks sway back and forth. They live more than an hour from the beach, but on hot days the air still smells like salt water. The windows fog over with condensation. The girl turns to the TV, where the news plays a slow crawl of events that feel distant. She can understand the people but they don't look like anyone she knows. Their skin and teeth are too light. Their hair is held perfectly in place. They speak in a measured non-regional dialect.

The rainwater runs off the roof of the small house and down through gutters clogged with dead leaves and acorns, into the ground. In the yard, in a small depression over the septic tank, another puddle starts to form. Fire ants, lifted from their hill, float on top of the water, scrambling over each other, using their drowned comrades as life rafts. The rain is so heavy it bounces off the ground like a solid thing. It filters through the sand and clay and limestone, leaving behind its impurities, ending up in a system of underground caves that stretches beneath the house and for miles north and south and east. Caves that kill curious divers by the dozens, the corpses of young men and women lost forever in the waters of the Florida aquifer, crystal clear and cold, bubbling up from the ground at natural springs, swimming holes in the middle of the woods, pumped out through giant pipes for drinking water, bottled, shipped away to the corners of the country on tractor-trailers.

And sometimes, without warning, the limestone crumbles in on itself, a sinkhole opens in the middle of a street, or a living room, or a pond. If you were standing near the edge of one of these, you would hear the clumps of dirt falling, falling, splashing into a reservoir deep below the surface of the earth, the sunlight suddenly illuminating fossils that haven't seen the sky in hundreds of thousands of years, the ground beneath your feet suddenly feeling less stable; that could be you down there, you think, with the fossils and the chunks of sidewalk and the living room furniture and the small, surprised fish, finding yourself relocated to an unrecognizable ecosystem, sinking deeper into that clear water as the sunlight gets farther and farther away, nothing to hold on to, soon to be fossilized yourself, preserved forever, in a place too easy to forget.

PASCUA FLORIDA

DERRICK AUSTIN

If, as certain scientists believe, water remembers:
what does the first historian dream?

~~~

Star-beneath-the-Sea,   silver
ring inlaid with amber

crucifix, whose hand did you adorn? The hand
covered in dark hair

hacking through muck,
through muckish air.   Yes, for the fountain

that keeps men fit
for pleasure, the pleasure of spices and fabled fruit.

That hand writ Florida anew
on that day of resurrection:

pinks, blues, and blood
reds; Tequesta, Timucua, and Tocobaga,

living tribes turned palimpsest.

~~~

There's a secret to water, I thought watching you swim.
Tongues dissolve. Nothing settles.

Mornings, I lounge on the shore,
sipping something strong and secret.

One ritual abuts the other.
I want so much
to cling to this life.

I want so much to be released
from this scarred narrative.

History's braid: semen, tears, memory, and milk.
My breath trembles out—how often I come
to the white-petaled water thinking we had touched.

STORM

LINDSAY HUNTER

FICTION

Roy's work picnic was at the third best park in town, everyone in bright yellow company t-shirts unless you were a sig oth, which you knew right away because a plump woman in a child's headband called out *Sig oth! Got ourselves a sig oth, don't we?* She was the t-shirt distributor, the name checker, the god at the gate.

Sig oth? She asked me. Soft fries piled on a napkin oozed at her elbow. The sequined pink bow just above her left eyebrow flashed in the sun.

No, I said.

Roy was Candace's boyfriend. I was Candace's sister. The night prior Roy had asked me to come, as some kind of consolation for how the gear shift had knuckled into my back, over and over, until the flesh there was soft and pocketed with blood. *I really rammed you*, he said when I'd bent to pick the wad of my shirt up. His fingertip traced the perimeter of the bruise, then swirled in, like he meant to mix the colors there.

Family? The woman asked. She clicked her pen, *ticket, ticket*, it seemed to say.

Kind of, I said.

Roy worked in a bottling plant. He cleared the jams, pressed On, pressed Off. He liked to keep one earplug mushed in to his ear and the other dangling like chewed gum on a string. Because of that he often said What? What? when I hadn't said anything at all.

Candace won't be there, Roy said. His chin resting on my sternum. My heart clomping harder what with this new pressure, the way a veal cow must feel inside the box. We could hold hands and shit. Right out in the open. The other guys won't say two words about it.

Well, the woman said. She put her pen down, lining it up neatly with the edge of her checklist. I could see blue checkmarks all down the page. The woman adjusted her headband, pressing it deeper into her scalp. She felt for the bow, pinching and plucking at it like it could be made into a different shape.

Roy invited me? I said. I was already deciding to back away, say it was a mistake, get into my car and hope the seat hadn't already gotten hot enough to burn my thighs.

Oh, sugar, why didn't you say so? The woman ran the point of her pen down the list, found Roy's name, and checked it off. I'm sorry about the runaround, she said. We just can't have strangers coming in here, eating our hot dogs. She looked up at me and winked, that relentless bow catching the sun and setting off a flurry of its own winks. Ogling our children, she added, cupping her doughy hand to her mouth, like only we were aware of the recent plague of child-ogling. A small silver watch tortured her wrist, tight as a rubber band.

Go on in, she said. Roy's back there somewhere.

The picnic was in the less woodsy part of the park, with orange clay dust rising up and clumps of weeds crackling underfoot and a big tire swing careening over the small pond that everyone called The Lake. There were three picnic tables in the dirt, and someone had drug folding chairs and an old coffee table out there. Aluminum pans of potato salad, bean salad, rice salad, fruit salad. Two smoking grills that a man in an enormous white cowboy hat traveled between, leaning forward and shrugging his shoulders the way people do when they want to look like they're running but are really just shuffling slowly across the dirt. Children in rubber sandals and diapers and dripping bathing trunks. Yellow shirted men throwing a Frisbee, passing a joint, laying in the weeds with forearms across their eyes. The women seemed to have all gathered in the covered area, perched among the picnic tables and yelling Hey at the children.

A man with Roy's hair stood down by the lake, bringing a beer up to his face, but then he turned and I could see that he had a mustache, glasses, was not Roy.

Hey, one of the women said. It was hard to tell which one had said it; they were all looking at me now.

Hey, I said.

There's white wine, the voice said again. You seem like a white wine kind of gal. The women laughed, loud and teasing, the way Candace laughed when she got drunk and started in on me.

Oh, no thanks, I said. I like beer.

The women didn't answer, but they shifted, relaxing.

Have y'all seen Roy? I asked. There was an empty spot between a woman whose belly lay on itself in layers, like a melting ice cream cone, and an old woman wearing a denim skirt and holding her purse to her heart.

Oh, he's around here somewhere, a voice said. It seemed like it was coming from a woman with a pyramid of dark curls atop her head. The women suddenly erupted into a chorus of Heys, some of them half leaving their seats, slamming their cups down on tables, Hey Hey Hey. One of the children was getting up, brushing its knees off. Another child had its mouth open in a silent scream, its fists frozen at its hips. Then the child released a wail, a shocked and heartbroken howl. Goddammit, Petey, one of the women said. One by one they sat, gathered up their cups again. The children wandered off, together, one wailing and one silent.

It's fixin to rain, the old lady said. It was easier to tell whose voice was whose. My eyes felt adjusted to that oddness of standing in the sunlight and looking into the dark of the covered area. I did not want to join the women, but I also did not want to join the men.

I believe it, Pyramid Head said.

The sky was taking on a greenish hue, the color heralding a rageful thunderstorm, probably about fifteen minutes off.

It'll come and go, the woman with the belly said. You know how it is.

Roy, huh? Another woman was looking at me, a woman in a black tank top with thick silver rings on each finger.

Yeah, you know where I can find him?

The woman shrugged. It ain't that big a place, she said. Where's Candy?

Candy's my sister, I said, as if that explained it. She had a shift, I added.

Roy was a joker, just the type of guy to invite someone to a picnic and then not show. He was probably parked outside my apartment, grinning, waiting for me to walk up. He liked to show up unannounced. He didn't know I was always conjuring him, telling the heat, the night, the thick air to bring him.

Candy's a good girl, someone said, and the women mmm'ed and hummed in agreement.

We could hold hands, Roy said. I didn't tell him I didn't even want to hold hands. I had already touched more than his hands. Holding hands would be a step back. My legs itched, my feet in a soup inside my shoes. The sky looked the color of a sick man's face. Sometimes Roy called me Little Sister. Oh, Little Sister. His rough chin on my belly, scraping the insides of my thighs. And then sometimes he acted like we were just two people. He'd get angry about a parking space. Or he'd ask me to lend him a dollar. Or he'd shift to his side to fart in his seat.

The sky rumbled, a polite throat clearing. Thunder, I said.

Naw, the woman in the rings said. I didn't hear it.

One of the children was beside me, its foot on my foot. A sticky hand worked its way into mine. The child swung from my hand, mashing my toes as it pivoted. It hollered, a shrieking whoo that bared all its teeth, square and evenly spaced and yellow at the back.

Tire swing, it yelled.

Naw, the woman said again.

I want her to do the tire swing with me, the child said.

Suit yourself, the woman said. She rubbed a hand on her arm, inspecting it, then pinched the flesh like she'd found a pimple.

I can't swim, I said.

It ain't deep, the old lady said. It's up to your thithers, that's all. The women hummed again. It seemed clear they welcomed distractions for the children. The lake, the tire swing, the whipping of charred meat into the tree line, the pushing and shoving in a cloud of dirt, the bossing a stranger around.

I don't want to, I said. Or maybe I will, I said, once the child began to holler again, after I find Roy.

Roy ain't here, the child said. He went off with Miss Cheryl—

To get more beer, Pyramid Head said.

Miss Cheryl? It felt like the only thing to do, was say her name again. The women nodded, moving their feet on the sandy concrete, tsk tsk tsk.

Yeah, the child said. My mama says Miss Cheryl got tig ol bitties.

Petey, his mama said, her voice like gravel in a blender. It ain't like that, she said to me, her voice smooth as icing now. We all know Roy's only got eyes for Candy.

Oh, I'm not worried about Candace, I said.

Candace always had boyfriends. One after another, like the streetlamps on the highway. I was on the side where they'd all burned out, nothing but darkness stretching this way and that. Had to walk across the median and pull one down toward me, put his hand on my tig ol bitty. When in darkness, find the light. That's in the Bible, or it should be.

Let's *go*, the child said.

I can't swim, I said again, but I let the child pull me toward the lake. My shoes bit at my ankles. They were the wrong kind of shoes to wear to a place like this and I let them fly off behind me as the boy yanked me along. My feet were caked in the dust when we reached the dock.

The man I had mistaken for Roy steadied the tire swing. Climb on up, he said. He was missing a tooth right in front but he wore it well, like he had too many teeth to begin with.

I stood in the tire and held the rope like I'd seen others do it before me. My hands began to ache. The rope was hard and rough and I was gripping it; even as I told my hands to loosen up I gripped even tighter.

You coming? I said to the child, but it backed away, shaking its head, yelling No as if it had been struck.

I knew you wouldn't do it, Petey, his mama yelled, and the child took off in a run, dust clouding up behind its feet like the child was evaporating.

Okay, girlie, the man said. Enjoy the ride. He pulled the tire back and let it go. The rope was short and I swung only so far before I was over the dock again. I could see a man by the lady with the bow, and another man rising up on his elbows. Neither were Roy. I closed my eyes and waited, the wind at the back of my head and then on my face. There she goes again, one of the men said. Someone whistled. The wind at the back of my head and then on my face. It really was simple as that, the conjuring. I opened my eyes and there Roy was, walking over from around the tatty volleyball net, watching me, that smile on his face like he forgot my name but it was no big deal, it didn't matter to him at all. The stone-colored sky seeped in just behind him, like he pulled the storm on a kite. I smiled back. I really couldn't swim. I had never learned. But I wanted to show Roy something, so I let go.

A STUDY OF HUMAN RESPONSES TO MAN-MADE DISASTER

SARAH GERARD

ESSAY

My first session at the oil spill conference was called "Sharing Oil Spill Science With Non-Scientists: Effectively Communicating Complex Research Results through Outreach and Educational Programs." The packet, given to each person when they came through the door, opened with bullet-pointed directions for how to conduct conference calls. The projector at the front of the room lit up and a woman with shiny blonde hair approached the podium to fiddle with the controls.

I had signed up for the conference in 2016 believing that it could help me write about the 2010 Deepwater Horizon oil spill. I was living in St. Petersburg, Florida when it happened, and although no oil washed up on our coast, there was a sense that something personal to us had come under threat. We gathered facts and signed petitions. We watched the news obsessively. No amount of information could shake the feeling of powerlessness wrought by the onslaught of images delivered to us by the media. The inferno of the blowout. The arterial spew from the wellhead. The torment of oiled animals. The disaster continued.

I grew up on the Gulf of Mexico. Some of my earliest memories involve the taste of saltwater. The spill left an indelible mark on my psyche. I had already been living in Brooklyn for six years when the conference came to Tampa, but I signed up looking for language to describe that scar, and when I opened the schedule, this session spoke to me. It seemed to tell a subtler story than the one in the news.

The woman with shiny blonde hair flashed a nuclear smile from the podium. "I'm Laura," she said. "I'm the Public Programs Specialist for the Smithsonian Marine Station." Laura's talk was called "Helping Scientists Effectively Share Their Science" and her message was to break free of the lecture format and find different ways to engage our audience. "There is no such thing as a general audience," she said. "Everyone has their life experience and things that make them who they are."

"We take it for granted that we know what scientists do, but not everyone does," she continued. "People want to know how somebody got to where they are and why they're doing what they're doing. Contrast your message: analytical content versus emotional content."

She passed around sets of blue and red Post-its and told us she was going to show us how to amplify the signal and reduce the noise on our research messages. She instructed us to break into four roughly equal-sized groups. We moved to the four corners of the room, where large pieces of paper hung taped to the walls, each bearing a heading: Audience, Message, Delivery, and Practice/Feedback. Red Post-its were for problems; blue Post-its were for solutions. We were told to start with our problems. We were in the Message corner.

A woman in the Audience corner raised her hand: "For logistical purposes, do you have to put each question or each suggestion on a separate—"

"No, you can list more than one," said Laura.

The room fell silent. Slowly, the corners began to murmur amongst themselves.

"You can remain anonymous in your problems and obstacles," said Laura. "This is a safe space."

•

I left Florida the first time when I went to college. It was 2003. I'd just turned eighteen and I was ready to leave it behind forever. I considered my hometown of Largo provincial. I agreed with people when they described my home state as crazy. Florida Man wasn't yet a hashtag because there was no Twitter, but Florida had a reputation. It was common—compared to New York, where I was now going to make my home. I had also become aware of the subtle ways in which my home state had seduced me, given me a too-heavy dose of fantasy— given outsiders an unrealistic idea of what life could be: Disney, spa days, nightclubs, nudist resorts. I objected to the chintziness of it, the materialism, the privilege: the whole of it felt like an empty gesture.

New York City had history to back up its claims to authenticity, I thought. Its architecture, its culture, had stood the test of time. I saw the city first when I visited colleges as a high school junior. I saw it the second time when I moved there. I never wanted to leave again.

But four years later, in 2007, in my last semester of college, I moved back to Florida to go to rehab for anorexia. I spent two weeks at my parents' house in Largo prior to checking in, gaining weight to meet the minimum requirement, as the rehab center didn't have medical staff on site. I passed the days attempting to drink Campbell's drinkable soups from the can. I rarely went outside.

When I did, I looked at the water. My parents' house is steps from the Intracoastal Waterway, a narrow channel that follows the coast of the U.S. from Boston, Massachusetts to Brownsville, Texas. As a child, I would reach the Intracoastal by slipping past the gate of my neighbor's private dock at nighttime, when I knew he wouldn't see me. I'd dangle my feet over the edge of the wood planks and watch the headlights of cars trace the causeways toward the beaches. I'd listen to the lap of the water against the pilings. I'd smell the vegetal aroma of mangroves and salt. Whatever churned inside me became still.

The beaches sit just across the Intracoastal, connected to the mainland every few miles. As a teenager, twice, I jumped off of the

Belleair Causeway because my friends dared me to, and swam back to land fully clothed, laughing hysterically, afraid of nothing—a Florida child passing the time. Now I rode my mother's bicycle over the Causeway to the shore. I laid it on the sand and sat, staring into the sun's glint on the water, hating that I was back in Florida, hating the reason why I was back there. I considered myself a failure.

Six weeks later, I returned to the beach with ten other women who were also learning to eat. I brought a book about Buddhist meditation, which I sat drowsily reading on the sand. One of the social workers, a priest, had given it to me, along with a ring engraved with Sanskrit prayers, which I was now wearing on my left middle finger. I turned it a circle, and felt the salt and sand beneath it.

I was in the Message group. We worked together to sort duplicate problems and duplicate solutions, and then match the questions to appropriate answers. The most common question was how many times you have to repeat your message. "Seven times," someone joked.

"I think it's interesting that nobody had suggestions for how to distill a complex message," one woman observed.

"People get caught up in the language they use all the time," said Beth, our facilitator and a science education consultant. "Scientists use this complex language because it elevates them in the eyes of their peers. They might not even know what words they don't consider jargon, that we'd consider jargon."

"Talking about most of what our researchers do is just not interesting to anyone," came a voice from the back of the group. Everyone moved to the side. A petite brunette with wavy hair and plastic-framed glasses looked back at us. Her nametag identified her as Kendra. "You have to make them understand why it's important to them. You like to eat fish? Microbes are very important to that. How does knowing about phytoplankton matter to you? Well, phytoplankton and microbes are the bottom of the food web."

We pondered this.

When it came time for my team to present what we'd discussed to the larger group, no one stepped up so Beth stepped in. "There are a few large issues scientists face in communicating their messages effectively," she said to the room, "and a few recurring themes, but the largest is using language that non-scientists don't understand."

Laura asked whether we'd identified a good solution for that.

"Yeah, do we have to explain every piece of information that our audience doesn't understand?" asked a woman in the Feedback group, looking deflated.

"Or just simplify the message," Laura suggested.

My plan had been to stay in rehab for sixty days and then move to Chicago to live with my boyfriend. I'd been living on Long Island and hated it for many of the reasons I'd hated Florida, its materialism, shallowness, and social conservatism among them. I felt more certain than ever that there was nothing left for me in Florida. I was ashamed at having had to move back. But I had serious reservations about moving to Chicago. Now that I'd taken my first shaky steps toward recovery, the extent of my boyfriend's alcoholism was apparent. Days before I checked out of rehab, he asked me what he would do now that I was healthy—where would that leave him, given that he was still an alcoholic? For selfish reasons, he didn't want me to recover. I was facing a problem of life or death, and if I wanted to live, I had to leave him.

Two months after leaving rehab, just weeks before I was set to move to Chicago, I broke up with my boyfriend. I had reunited with the cousin of a best friend, whom I'll call Michael. He was addicted to cocaine but preferred the lighter and the needle to his nose. He was also newly clean and just as eager as I was to get out of Florida. The train-hopping subculture was strong in St. Petersburg. Wayward kids would come and go with the seasons, gathering up in public parks, intermingling with the rest of us. We found one of them to give us a "crew change" guide—an underground document passed around by hobos.

For two moths, we hitchhiked and rode trains up the east coast. We stopped in Rockland, Maine, and spent a few weeks living with his uncle, painting his house and riding bikes to the harbor. We walked out into the mud in bare feet. We hitchhiked back down south to Worcester, Massachusetts, where we hopped our last train.

We rode for ten hours, through the night, in the rain. The last thing I remember just before I hit the ground the next morning, pulling into the Buffalo rail yard, is the gravel rushing toward my face. I got a hundred and fifty stitches and lost a tooth. My parents came to get me. I ended up back in St. Petersburg once again.

St. Petersburg sits on the end of a peninsula. Drive far enough in most any direction, you'll hit the water. Back in St. Petersburg, Michael and I moved in together. I called him my boyfriend. On the weekends, we'd visit my parents in Largo and, after dinner, drive over the causeway to Indian Rocks Beach and look out at the dusk-cloaked Gulf of Mexico. One night, as we did this, he said he had something to tell me.

"It's about Charleston," he said, "when I took our money and went to buy weed."

He had left me sitting at a gas station and gone off with a stranger he met loitering by the bathrooms. I sat on a patch of grass with our packs, repairing them with dental floss. He was gone for over an hour. I had no way to know where he was, our cell phones were dead, and he didn't have his with him, anyway—it was in his pack, with me. When he returned, he looked ill. His face was pale and sweaty. He was breathing heavily. I asked him what was wrong but he wouldn't say.

That night, we'd slept in a wooded area below the freeway. A creek ran through it and lightly babbled as we strung up our tarp, lay our sleeping bags down, and rested our heads on our arms. I had forgotten about that night.

"I bought crack," he told me now, looking out at the Gulf. "I regret it."

He turned toward me and I searched for his pupils in the dark. I imagined him looking back at me: the bright pink scar bisecting my face, the swelling around my left cheekbone, my crooked glasses. For a long time, the waves were the only sound.

"I wanted to be honest with you," he said.

A presentation on plankton and larval anchovy was already underway when I arrived at the "Physiological Resiliency of Marine Fish and Invertebrates Following Oil Exposure" session. I was starting to wonder about this word 'resilience'—I'd heard it again and again and it seemed like everyone had a different definition for it but felt defining it was unnecessary. The Deepwater Horizon spill happened during anchovy spawning season. Somehow the presence of oil-exposed plankton was generating toxicity for the larval anchovies: the "plankton effect." The consequences were clear: larvae warped by curved spines, deformed yolk sacs, missing eye buds. "These deformities are ultimately fatal to the larvae," said the presenter.

I conducted an informal survey of scientists eating lunch in the hotel lobby. "Resilience is writing a fifteenth grant proposal after your first fourteen got rejected," one said.

"I think resilience is the ability to rebound and come back to being normal and healthy again."

"For me, if you have some biological community, like phyto-plankton, and that becomes impacted, how long is it before they bounce back to their original state?"

"Resiliency depends on context, but I think what it's actually re-ferring to is: animals which have short life histories, high reproductive rates—lots of eggs, so to speak—and the population turns over fast, are more resilient because they can withstand a high level of impact. Most of them die naturally."

"Resilience is somewhat timescale- and spatial scale-dependent, like all science. It's the ability of a system to withstand perturbation without altering itself significantly. You could perturb the system and you've changed it, but it will return to its original state. It was affected but the effect was temporary."

A man with a kind mouth and a salt-and-pepper beard put his hand on my shoulder and looked me in the eye. "In the world I work with, resilience is not bouncing back, it's bouncing forward. If you bounce back, you're already behind again. You will be behind again when stuff happens."

When our lease expired, Michael went out train hopping again. I stayed in Florida. We'd sometimes talk on the phone. He was angry that I didn't come with him and told me he was living in a squat house in New Orleans, which I assumed meant he was using again. I'd moved in with a friend in a two-bedroom house in a historic neighborhood. We had an organ in the parlor, and a fireplace, and a cat. I got a job as a line cook at a restaurant downtown. On weekends, the men in the efficiency next door would grill hot dogs and drink Coronas and blast Van Morrison from a little handheld radio next to my window. I had finished all of the surgeries to replace my lost tooth and was growing my hair out to hide the more awkward angles of my face, still swollen from the accident— the swelling would subside over a matter of years, I was told. I was told to massage it.

I started dating an artist who strung me along. He was someone I'd dated briefly years before and he knew that I loved him. I felt the kind of longing for him that you only find in literature. I showed up at the art gallery where he worked. I left presents on his doorstep. I needed something from him, but I didn't know that. We fucked on the rug in his studio and in his '63 Volkswagen Squareback, and he drove me over the Sunshine Skyway one night with a joint when he knew I was sad about him. He knew how to win me over. He was fundamentally incapable of showing it, but I knew he loved me, too. I could feel it in his touch. I could hear it in the way he said my name.

One night, we drove down to Pass-a-Grille, to an unoccupied beach that had become our favorite: all duplexes and stilt houses and beach bars and no one else around when the sun went down.

We left our clothes on the sand and climbed out onto the wave breakers to lower ourselves in, leaning slowly into the swells. He swam out first and I swam out after him. We let go of each other and floated free: this was how he was, I thought. He likes to be alone.

I closed my eyes and turned my belly to the sky. When I opened them, he was gone, and so was the shoreline.

The wave breakers were gone. I'd drifted too far out. There was blackness all around me and the sound of the wind and the sound of distant waves breaking against the sand, but the sound seemed to come from everywhere.

I called his name. I called again. I called again.

I closed my eyes and again turned my belly to the sky. I visualized the shoreline. The water leeching from the sand, pulled back out to sea. The creatures in the sand that retreated with the water. I visualized arriving safely on top of it. I imagined the artist was a magnet and I the iron.

I slammed against the wave breakers and opened my eyes to water. I rolled over and covered my head with my arms, and scrambled up the jagged rocks tasting blood in my mouth. I called his name.

Porfirio was eating lunch with his wife and invited me to sit with them. He's an older man, well-dressed, with a warm demeanor. "We refer to our ecosystems in terms of how these systems can return to their original state, or how you can keep them in their original state," he said. "However, we also know that the word has been used by economists—in economic terms, to be 'resilient.' And also for people living, in this case, in coastal areas."

Porfirio lives in the Tabasco state of Mexico. Tabasco is below sea level with a watershed. In 2007, heavy rainfall from an offshore system caused a dam to break, flooding Tabasco and Chiapas in what was one of the worst natural disasters in the country's history. Over 20,000 residents were forced to seek emergency shelter, and over a million people were affected—more than half of Tabascans.

"How to bring back all the people, and the economy, and everything to—not to the original state, because that's impossible—but how can you help people and the communities to be more strong?" Porfírio said. "To enhance their strength, to resist collapse and to return somehow?"

Mexico has another serious concern: its wetlands and mangroves. Other sectors, such as tourism, are competing with local ecosystems. "They're trying to sell the clean, blue ocean to people, to go there and to stay in a nice hotel," he said. "But they build hotels on top of mangroves and sand dunes, and they destroy the nature. This is not a resilient way to do business."

To build a road or hotel in the middle of an ecosystem is to destroy the ecosystem by fragmenting it. Even if sections of it remain, they won't be able to survive because they're interdependent but no longer connected. Once a road is built through a mangrove, soon other roads will be built to connect with it. Once a hotel appears on a virgin beach, soon other hotels will spring up around it. With time, the whole ecosystem will disappear.

"That's the problem that people in other sectors don't understand," said Porfírio. "Nature needs to be strong and well-conserved, and preserved, so that it's functional. If we fragment an ecosystem or a habitat, it's not resilient."

The solution could be as easy as elevating the road by building it on pillars, he said. That way, the wetland remains intact.

"You have to take into consideration that wetlands move and they survive because of water," he said, "and that if you put a road there without these considerations, and you block the water flowing, you kill the whole ecosystem, not just the portion where you built the road. So, to be resilient means to be strong—but it also means to give the opportunity for strength to other people, those coming yet in the future."

·

I'd already prepared to leave Florida again when the oil spill happened. I'd spent three years there rebuilding and redefining myself: what I wanted from my life, what I was capable of, what I no longer wanted to claim as part of my identity. I supported myself as a freelance journalist. I made a new group of friends with whom I went to the beach a few times a week: if one of us was having a shitty day, if we needed a tan, just because. We went skinny dipping at night when the sharks were out and the water was warm and the lights of hotels died on the sand. My favorite beaches were the ones farther south on the peninsula, with names like Sunset and Treasure Island, and farther south Fort de Soto, and farther south Sanibel.

I was moving to New York City in a matter of weeks to go to grad school. In the meantime, I'd continue to write for local papers, arts and culture stories and small-scale human-interest pieces. Nothing hard-hitting. I was a good writer, but I had limited credentials and a limited beat.

St. Petersburg had come to stand in some ways for the primary trauma of my life. It was the price I paid for the stupidest mistake, the place I'd been delivered to when I was at my lowest. I understood it too well, felt too attracted to its slower pace, its laid-back culture, its vacationland aesthetic. It was a version of myself that embarrassed me. I was afraid that if I stayed there any longer, I'd stay forever. I had worked my way almost out of it and I needed to leave for good.

When the wellhead blew, I was sitting in a bookstore coffee shop struggling to make headway on several pieces I was writing simultaneously to puzzle together rent. I stared at the TV transfixed, watched the muddy black spread across the surface of the water. I watched the fire raging on the platform. I scoured the Internet for any and all information, attempting to devise a plan for getting myself to ground zero. I cried angry, powerless tears. I was ready to leave

Florida, but Florida would always be a part of me, and that part of me had been deeply wronged.

Over the weeks that followed, oiled birds arrived at our local sanctuary. Volunteers traveled north to clean our neighbors' beaches. The rest of us watched and waited and mourned. It was true that we'd done this to ourselves, on some level, but we couldn't have foreseen the devastation.

The coastline of the Gulf of Mexico stretches from Florida to the Yucatan and along Cuba. The Gulf's deepest point is a 14,383-foot trough, or about two and three-quarters miles deep, though half of the Gulf consists of the shallow waters of the continental shelf, which is where the oil spill happened: forty-one miles off the coast of Louisiana, at a mile's depth, which made stopping it nearly impossible. The number of active drill sites in the Gulf of Mexico has gone down significantly, from almost half of those offshore worldwide in 2000 to twenty percent in 2008. But exploration is moving into deeper and more dangerous waters. We're now drilling at two miles' depth.

The Gulf formed 300 million years ago, in the Late Triassic period, with the breakup of Pangea. The continent split to form what would become North and South America. Originally the Gulf was much larger: as far north as Oklahoma and as far west as west Texas. Then the basin filled in along the margins with sediment to form land.

Most people don't know that oil spills happen in the Gulf of Mexico all the time. If they aren't a certain size, or don't leave a sheen on the surface of the water, the industry isn't required to report them. The Gulf is an enormous body of water, and the idea is that small spills get diluted.

Deepwater Horizon was a volume of oil the industry had never seen. The ecological and toxicological effects were unknown for everyone. The psychosocial complexities of the spill were equally dire. I heard a story about a shrimping family in New Orleans: the husband was out of work during the year that the fisheries were shut down, and his wife told the researcher, "I'm not used to him being home at this time of year." She was used to having alone time with her kids, and having time for herself at night. "He's not happy that he can't work," she said. "And I'm used to having this time for me."

Nearly a third of the seafood harvested in the U.S. comes from the coastal zone of Louisiana. Most of those commercial fish and shellfish species depend on estuaries and marshes at some point during their life cycle. Many of the marshes around New Orleans are still full of oil. No one knows for sure how to get rid of it. It might go away on its own, but on a geological timescale, not a human one. On that scale, the ocean is resilient. Nature is resilient.

The poster session was a madhouse. Rows upon rows of Velcro display boards filled the lower level of the convention center. "Effects of 2- and 6-hydrolated Chrysene on the Development of Danio rerio Embryos," one read. "High Frequency Multibeam Sonar Water Column Backscatter: A 3D View of Water Column Acoustic Anomalies to Facilitate Ecosystem Science." "The Relative Potency of Methylated Chrysenes in Aryl Hydrocarbon Receptor (AhR) Activation." Scientists talked animatedly about hydrophobic liquid studies and the use of semi-permeable membrane devices and scyphozoan jellyfish. I walked up and down the aisles in a daze.

Finally, I found a poster that called to me: "Five Years Later: Determining Public Perception of Community Recovery and Post-Crisis Management Following the Deepwater Horizon Oil Spill." The presenter was a friendly-looking blonde in a skirt suit. She introduced herself as Angela, an assistant professor at the University of Florida, and said she was involved in helping communities become more resilient in the face of disasters.

They wanted to know, in particular, how these individuals and communities felt about the spill's impacts on their lives, and whether the spill continued to impact their lives today. Angela works with communities that are very connected to the surrounding ecosystem and rely on it for their livelihood. She was currently working closely with Apalachicola, Florida to develop a disaster response playbook identifying the twelve different people needed in the wake of a disaster to determine what should be done and how, specifically in the cases of man-made disasters.

"We heard time and time again from individuals in these areas, 'We can handle a natural disaster; we know what to do. We have our tools and can rebuild a house. But Deepwater Horizon was different. We felt like we were sitting on our hands waiting for oil to reach our coast,'" Angela said.

I related to this. Growing up in Tampa Bay, there was always some terrible storm threatening to make landfall. We'd stock up on food and candles, X-tape the windows, fill up the bathtub, and sit tight until it passed. As adults, my friends and I would throw beer-soaked "hurricane parties"—threats of hurricanes were no big deal. But when Deepwater Horizon happened, all we could do was watch, like watching a loved one die slowly from cancer—there was nothing we could do to save the Gulf. The sight of it alone was a wound. I asked Angela what it is about the water that makes us feel so elementally connected with it.

"I had this conversation with someone in Apalachicola once," she said. "They told me, 'I have to live near the water because it's my faith. It's my solace. If something's gone wrong, I go and sit by the water. It's my way to reconnect to what's important.'"

SIXTH WONDER

KEVIN MOFFETT

FICTION

I've been watching the nest cam again. The eaglets hatched and the mother eagle sits atop them and waits, like I wait, for the father eagle to return with a fish. On screen next to the nest cam is a live chat between a biology class and a wildlife expert. Questions appear quicker than the expert can reply to them. A student writes, Doesn't look like they made their nest right *at all*. And it's true, the nest does seem sort of lopsided. I used to wait for the father because when the mother moved to feed the eaglets it allowed a better look at them, wobbly and covered in gray down. Lately, I'm more interested in the father's catch. The fish is alive when he drops it into the nest and I imagine the feeling of being plucked from a river by expert talons, pulled from one element into a new one. Air, the first failure of my equipment. I bet it would feel like birth, cruel but important, and while eagles tore at my flesh, I'd be nostalgic not for the water but for the moment I was removed from it, when I flew. How had I not known I could fly? I'd be thinking.

My mother never told me storks delivered babies but she did say yes when I asked if she'd ever given a blow job. I was eight and didn't know what a blow job was—I must have overheard the phrase in school and asking if she'd given one (actually, I think I said *done* not *given*, had she ever done a blow job) was a way of asking exactly what one was. She never did tell me. For years my proxy definition of blow job was: something my mother has given, something my mother has done. To be perfectly honest the phrase blow job still conjures stubborn memory wisps of my mother. I'm thinking of her now. In the morning she'd ask my sister and me what details we remembered from our dreams, and if we said being trapped in a castle or something, she'd flip through her dream dictionary and interpret what our unconscious minds were hiding, never anything very good. Plus I could tell she left stuff out. As a teenager my sister stopped telling our mother her dreams but I never did. I started telling lies instead.

Whose little boy are you? she used to say when she was tired of me. Her eyes scanning my face without recognition, a menu of foods she didn't want in a language she didn't speak. Shouldn't you go look for your mommy?

I hated that. Whenever I remind her about it she acts like she doesn't remember. I bring it up more often than I should. My mother calls and we watch the nest cam together, her in Florida, me in California. She demands so little of me now—a phone call every two weeks, a card on her birthday, a silencing of past grievances—but I still have a hard time giving it to her. Talking to her makes me impatient, inversely annoyed with whatever she's excited about, even the nest cam. She and my sister fought over a dollhouse a few years ago and now my sister calls her *that woman* and rarely visits her. I never thought you'd turn out to be the normal one, my mother often tells me.

When I was in elementary school she chaperoned a trip to Blue Springs to visit our class manatee, Randy. For months we wrote him letters, but all he sent were fun facts (Fun Fact! All my teeth are molars!) and autographed photos. It's not even his signature, one of my classmates said disgustedly. We were excited anyway. When we arrived the guide pointed to a listless herd of manatees, ancient as dinosaur eggs in the clear water, and asked which was ours. Our teacher told him and the guide said, Oh, I'm so sorry. Randy died a few nights ago.

He said it with such enthusiasm I thought he was joking. He went on about industrial contaminants and the delicate ecosystem of the spring. Kids who weren't afraid to cry cried. Others stared at the manatees. For some reason I reached for my mother's hand and held it. When it became clear that we were just going to hop back on the bus and leave, my mother let go of my hand, stamped over to the guide and said, You could've pointed to any of those fat-ass manatees and said there's Randy and nobody would've known the difference.

I can't recall if he was defensive or chagrined, but neither he nor the teacher could placate her. Finally she said, We want a new one. Today. We're not going anywhere until that happens. The guide left and we sat at picnic tables and ate bag lunches, thinking about Randy and his fun facts. The guide returned a half-hour later with a picture of our new manatee, Tammy. Point her out, my mother said.

The guide indicated where Tammy was floating and told us how special she was because she'd already given birth twice. Back in class, though, Randy's picture stayed on the wall and Tammy wasn't mentioned again. What did we learn on our trip to Blue Springs? our teacher asked. No one was sure.

My mother calls in the morning to tell me that the dead fish is still in the nest with the eagles. He spent all night there, head intact, body picked clean. First, water, then air, then a crooked bed of twigs. I'm going to die without any idea what I'm capable of. This is what I'd be thinking, as eagles fed me to other eagles.

GUTTED

LIDIA YUKNAVITCH

ESSAY

One

The largemouth bass is an olive-green fish. In the North East right after ice-out, it most often has a gray color, marked by a series of dark, sometimes black, blotches forming a jagged horizontal stripe along each flank. The upper jaw of a largemouth bass extends beyond the rear margin of the orbit. In comparison to age, a female bass is larger than a male. The largemouth bass is the state freshwater fish of Florida. The fish lives 16 years on average.

I'm sixteen and we move from the cool, rain-soaked evergreen mountains of Washington state to the sinkholes and sand and heat wet of Florida. I can't breathe right. The air is too thick, too heavy, carrying some trace of a colonizing history, or just the weight of father that I can finally name. My father's story is that we moved to Gainesville, Florida for me. For my swimming career. So that I could train with Randy Reese at Florida Aquatic Swim Team. That's what he tells me over and over again. It's a sacrifice. For me.

In reality, he is transferred from his job at CH2M Hill from Washington state to Florida, where he will be lead architect in their engineering firm. It's a step up for him.

More money. More prestige. Bigger projects. But that is not the story he tells his daughter.

Why do fathers tell their daughters lies that they have to carry the rest of their lives? What is the weight of father on a daughter?

He is no longer abusing me. I am very strong. Swimmer strong. I am away from the house a lot. Swimming. I am filled with a rage muscling up my biceps and thighs. Almost animal. My eyes are steel blue. When he stares at me I don't flinch. Anymore.

No one knows what our next moves will be.

Two

Largemouth bass are keenly sought after by anglers and are noted for the excitement of their fight. The fish will often become airborne in their effort to throw the hook, but many say that their cousin species, the smallmouth bass, can beat them pound for pound. Large golden shiners are a popular live bait used to catch trophy bass, especially when they are sluggish in the heat of summer or in the cold of winter. Largemouth bass usually hang around big patches of weeds and other shallow water cover. These fish are capable of surviving in a wide variety of climates and waters. They are perhaps one of North America's most tolerant fish.

The first week of high school in Gainesville, Florida, two alarming things happen to me. The first thing is accidental. I am standing too near a girl brawl in the hallways between classes. I'm the only white girl there in that moment. I'm new. I haven't figured out where to stand, what to do with my hands, how to carry my body through the rivered hallways of this new place. I sweat too much because my clothes are not Florida yet. I smell like chlorine. I get punched in the nose, clocked a good one, hard enough that I fall to the ground. Next to no one notices—nothing about the girl brawl has a single thing to do with me. I was just a body in the way, a face that connected with a fist. Even though at sixteen I don't yet know a god damn thing, like my father tells me all the time, I know this: take it.

My eyes well up and my nose and skull hurt and all I see is feet. Down there on the ground. But I do. I take it. I say nothing. I get up quietly and walk away. I have nothing to do with the action, the characters, the story. I go into the bathroom and lock myself in a stall and cry, but only a little. When I go to French class my teacher asks me what on earth happened to my nose and eyes, which must be starting to turn colors. "Nothing," I say, and bury my face in my books.

The second thing that happens the first week of high school is that I fall in love completely with a boy swimmer. Not only is he on my swim team, but he is an artist, and art is my favorite place to be besides inside books or in water. I will spend every single day possible with this boy until the day I leave Florida to go to college. The boy becomes a world to me. A body that makes it possible to bear my own. The story doesn't go anywhere though. He will never love me. I haven't yet learned a god damn thing about love, mine or anyone's. I wouldn't know love if it punched me in the nose.

Three

How to gut a largemouth bass: Use a quality fish scaler to scale fish you are planning on cooking with their skin on. Remove the gills, guts and kidney as soon as possible because these spoil fast in a dead fish. You can remove the gills by cutting the throat connection and along both sides so that the gills pull out easily.

1. *Insert the knife blade in the belly and run it up to the gills.*
2. *Pull the guts and the gills out.*
3. *Cut the membrane along the backbone.*
4. *Scrape out the kidney and bloodline from underneath the membrane.*

I think it might be true that arriving in Florida was a leaving. I was already leaving the moment I got there; I hated it passionately. Those scant years, between high school and college, everything in me was about leaving. I left my father's house forever. I left my alcoholic mother. I left the boy I loved. I left the girl I was, the girl who did not know a god damn thing, in our garage next to my father's Camaro. I left ever being abused again—except that isn't true, is it—I found other fists later in life, I found other ways to punish myself when no one else was around to do it. And, the truth is, I left a bloodline near a sinkhole near my house in Florida.

The sinkhole is called Devil's Hole. The water was aquamarine. People used to be able to swim in it. Like I did. It also has an underwater cave system. I was swimming there with the boy I loved who would never love me when I started bleeding.

I bled late, likely due to competitive swimming workouts, running, and weight training six out of seven days a week. I was training with Randy Reese of F.A.S.T., after all. So the fact that my periods didn't show up until I was nearly seventeen is not as odd as it sounds. But I bled that day, and since no women anywhere including my mother or sister ever educated me about my own body, I thought I was dying of cancer. When I crawled out of the waters at Devil's Hole, between my legs blood rivered. The boy I loved said I turned white as a sheet, oh my god he said, white like a girl from Washington state, white like the white people who eventually consumed Florida.

The history of Florida can be traced back to when the first Native Americans began to inhabit the peninsula as early as 14,000 years ago. They left behind artifacts and archeological evidence. Written history begins with the arrival of Europeans to Florida; the Spanish explorer Juan Ponce de Leon in 1513 made the first textual records. The state was the first mainland realm of the United States to be settled by Europeans.

From that time of contact, Florida has had many waves of immigration, including French and Spanish settlement during the 16th century, as well as entry of new Native American groups migrating from elsewhere in the South, and free blacks and fugitive slaves, who became known as Black Seminoles. Florida was under colonial rule by Spain, France and Great Britain during the 18th and 19th centuries before becoming a territory of the United States in

1821. Two decades later, in 1845, Florida was admitted to the union as the 27th U.S. state. Since the 19th century, immigrants have arrived from Europe, Latin America, Africa and Asia.

Florida is nicknamed the "Sunshine State" due to its warm climate and days of sunshine, which have attracted northern migrants and vacationers since the 1920s. A diverse population and urbanized economy have developed. In 2011, Florida, with over 19 million people, surpassed New York and became the third largest state in population. In 2015, the percentage of white people was recorded at 77%. The American Indian population was recorded as .4% in 2010. The African American population was recorded at 16% in 2015. The Hispanic or Latino population was recorded at 24% in 2015.

The economy has developed over time, starting with natural resource exploitation in logging, mining, and fishing, as well as cattle ranching, farming, and citrus growing. The tourism, real estate, trade, banking, and retirement destination businesses followed.

I've not been able to go back since I left.

I don't know why.

Except that the heat and afternoon storms gave me headaches so bad I threw up.

Except that my mother tried to kill herself. Twice.

Except that I loved someone who was never going to love me back...at least not in the way that sixteen-year-old girls could understand, until I did.

Except that my last showdown in the garage with my father is an image emblazoned forever on my brain, his fist hanging suspended in the air like love gone wrong, my face so close, so close, so red and hot, my breathing caught in my lungs the moment before the rest of my god damn life.

MAJOR DISASSOCIATION ON CRESCENT LAKE

JEFF PARKER

What I'm looking for in a motel is squalor on the inside and some reasonably agreeable scenery on the out-. I like to stew in the squalor, and that's precisely what I was doing, stewing in the squalor of Monticello Inn room number eighteen, when someone knocked.

I opened the door. A girl with fat, blonde dreads straddled a black cruiser. The bike had a decent front basket, but the tires were worn, and mildew stained the obnoxious whitewalls. On the chain guard there was a picture of a blue Indian goddess, her pink tongue sticking out, and the word *Sheeba*. The girl wore a baggy pink shirt with slits cut all through it and low-ass jeans.

"You up for hanging out?" she said.

The whole point of coming back here was that I didn't know anyone anymore, but I have always been a sucker for company. "Hang on a sec," I said. I grabbed two near beers from the mini-fridge. They were warm when I put them in, and the fridge seemed to have heated them a little. We sat on the curb in front of room eighteen. "Where you coming from on that thing?" I asked.

"I'm coming from around," she said. "Where you coming from?"

"I'm coming back," I said. She let me ride her Sheeba bike. I tried a catwalk but went over backwards and the bike clanked across the asphalt. "I'm from around here, but I haven't been back in eighteen years."

"I'm eighteen," she said.

"I was your age when I left."

"Hey, you know what would be fun," I said. "Instead of telling me your name and doing this whole getting to know each other thing, why don't you pretend to be my ex-girlfriend Bregs. I haven't seen Bregs in eighteen years."

I had tried this many times before, usually with women who at least looked like Bregs, who had her kind of Mediterranean Hepburn thing. With her blonde dreads and pale skin, this girl looked nothing like Bregs.

"Like act?" the girl said. "What was this Bregs like?"

"She had the frame of a bird and the smile of a horse. She was your age last I saw her."

"You keep those beers coming, I'll be Queen of the Nile," she said.

The girl didn't seem to understand that the beer was not real beer. "Okay," I said. "Let's go for a walk, Bregs. I'll show you the reasonably agreeable scenery."

We leaned her Sheeba bike against the wall in my room. She dropped a thready, rasta-colored purse on the floor.

"Bregs would never put her bag on the floor," I said.

"Oh," she said. "Where would she put it?"

"On a table or on a chair or on the bed. She thought the floor was dirty. She had a very clear division in her mind of dirty versus clean."

The girl looked around. She picked up her purse and threw it on the bed. "Not sure where that bed comes in on dirty versus clean," she said.

"But it's not the floor," I said. "That would be Bregs' point. You should feel free to dial up the neurotic like that."

"Whatevs," she said. "Check."

Next to the Monticello Inn was Crescent Lake. It was shaped more like an amoeba than a crescent. Two old ladies sat in plastic chairs on the bank flinging bread at birds. Hundreds of birds. "A bird jamboree," I said. "A bird feeding frenzy. A bird fiesta."

"A bird bacchanal," the girl said. That was exactly something that Bregs would say.

"Very good," I said.

One of the ladies called a goose by the name Zsa Zsa. "Zsa Zsa, come here," she said. And Zsa Zsa came to her. Zsa Zsa was different than the other geese. The other geese looked like stuffed animals and bobbed side to side as they walked. The other geese had carrot-colored beaks. Zsa Zsa had a bulbous growth on her charcoal face.

A tall bird with an elephantitis head pecked at Zsa Zsa. "Mind your manners you, Shirley Feather," the old lady said to the tall bird with an elephantitis head.

Me and Bregs walked the trail circling the lake. It was exactly nine-tenths of a mile around.

"Well," she said, "what have you been up to these last eighteen years?"

"I traveled around some," I said. "Evidently, I was married, and so on."

"Same with *moi*," she said.

"Hey, do you remember the time your feral cat bit my hand," I said, "really sunk its fangs into the meat?" I showed her the little vampiric scars on my palm, and the girl's glance narrowed.

"Don't talk bad about a cat just because she bit you. That cat wasn't feral. That was a normal cat."

"He," I said.

"Just because he bit you," she said.

"I was carving a pumpkin. The pumpkin freaked the cat out."

"Honestly I don't remember that. I remember the cat but not any pumpkin or any him biting you."

"What about the time we were biking and I braked to miss a lizard and you swerved around and crashed into a tree? Or the time cops came to your apartment and I'd left out my weed?"

She shook her head strangely, half yes-nod half no-nod. "All I remember is washing dishes and the knife slicing my hand through the sponge." We walked another tenth of a mile in silence. "I hoped seeing you again might make me remember lots," she said. "It's not working though. All I'm getting out of this whole thing is major disassociation. Maybe I should go."

She pinched together the skin between her eyebrows so that a line appeared there. I didn't know if she was playing the part or seriously weirding out. On occasion, in the past, others who looked more like Bregs than her had weirded out.

We circled back around to the lady and the birds. Zsa Zsa hissed at us. A man raked scum out of the lake. The scum smelled fresh and exciting. Some anorexic white ibises needled the grass with their hooked red beaks. The sun set behind a massive Banyan tree with roots trunking from every branch. The light broke sharply across the lake, catching hundreds of little black triangles on the surface. Turtle heads.

I do not pine for Bregs. And I did not expect the girl to be a good her. I appreciate the opportunity to reminisce a little bit is all. It's interesting for me to compare someone in the role of Bregs to my memory of Bregs herself, who, if we're being honest, was not all that special. Probably Bregs would remember something like the knife slicing her hand through the sponge rather than her cat biting me. That was totally feasible Bregs. And it was nice to be back in the squalor with a feasible Bregs after all these years.

The view from Monticello Inn room number eighteen was a dryer exhaust in a cinder block wall. Black mold bloomed in the corners of the ceiling. Rust marks stained the pillowcases, and the bathroom door seemed to have been clawed apart. We bought a Styrofoam of nachos and drank mugs of green tea with hot water from the tap. She kissed my sweaty forehead.

"Green tea makes the breath fishy," she said. "Let's brush teeth."

She removed a zipper pouch from her rasta bag, which was now on the chair, and we went to the bathroom together. The splintered wood from the door caught on my t-shirt.

She brushed her teeth.

"I don't have a toothbrush," I said.

"Gross. Use mine."

She brushed her teeth and then I brushed my teeth with her wet toothbrush, and we lay our heads on the rusty pillows. The girl was flimsy but with a persistent there-edness. The hair at the bottom of her dreads frayed. Several of the dreads had wooden napkin holders around them.

"I don't want to alarm you," she said at a certain point, "but you have a bug on your face." I felt my face and found something. Blood smeared my finger.

"What is it?" I said. Because of the way she had approached this, in a very Bregs-like fashion, I was not alarmed.

She threw back the sheet. "They're all over us," she said. "Bedbugs!"

We jumped out of bed and slapped at ourselves. She snatched her rasta bag off the chair. She ran toward the door in her underwear.

"Stop," I said. "You have four on your back."

"Get them off."

I brushed off three of them. The fourth was stuck. I brushed at it a few times until I realized it was a mole.

She opened the door. "Where are you going?" I asked.

"You are too unfamiliar," she said. "I assumed you'd be familiar."

I swallowed. "At this stage," I said, "you might bring it down a touch."

"How is it possible that I don't even remember my cat biting you?"

"It's the middle of the night. It's nice with you here. I propose that we sleep on the furniture."

"On the furniture?" she said. She looked at the furniture. "Okay, on the furniture."

She poured more water over a green tea bag and dabbed it onto our welts.

We moved the TV from the dresser to the floor. I stretched out on the dresser, my feet hanging off. She curled into a fetal position on the round table in the middle of the room. She used her rasta bag as a pillow. She put the white bath towel over her body and the white hand towel over her feet.

I turned out the light. "See you later, alligator," she said. And I said, "After a while, Gomer Pyle."

I woke up before dawn. She was still curled on the round table. She had kicked off the hand towel. I put it back on her feet. She looked happy in her sleep. I walked to Amoeba Lake.

Many of the geese stood on one leg with their heads tucked between their wings. It was easy to make out Zsa Zsa even from a distance because the loose manner in which she held her wings reminded me of Freddy Kreuger.

I decided to walk another nine-tenths of a mile. Large creatures splashed in the lake. Things cooed and croaked there. Gangs of ducks warred in the blackness. Something monkeyish screeched from the Banyan tree.

The streetlights behaved like their motion sensors were installed backwards. If I stopped and stood still, they turned on, but if I moved they turned off again.

Every so often there was a bench and a dark figure sitting on the bench. Skinny upright shadows, their eggheads facing the lake. I wondered what all the figures were doing in the middle of the night.

At six-tenths of a mile, I noticed a structure on the water, nestled into the foliage of the Banyan tree. It hadn't been there earlier. It looked like a shack floating on fifty-gallon drums. I approached the shore. A man came out of the shack with a flashlight and stood on one of the fifty-gallon drums.

"Land, ho!" he said.

"What are you doing here?" I asked.

"Living," he said. "Come on aboard."

He extended a shaky wooden ladder from one of the fifty-gallon drums to the bank, and I walked across.

Aboard the boat, I sensed a hum. There was a door with a doorknob like on a regular house. He opened the door for me, and we went inside. A Christmas tree stood in the corner. It was nowhere near Christmas. I pulled off a needle to check if it was real. It was real.

"I like the scent of the holidays," he said. He picked up a guitar from a mattress in the corner and sat down at a rickety table cluttered with pens and wires and tools and tubes and matchbooks and an old IBM Thinkpad. "My name is Winston, like the cigarettes," he said.

I looked at a painting on the wall of the shack that was now a boat when it was just a regular house on the ground. I felt even less safe than I usually feel. I sat down in the chair across from him.

He had long hair in a ponytail and a high forehead. He strummed and sang: "Nobody knows the trouble I seen. Nobody knows the places I bean. Nobody knows the places I seen. Nobody knows the trouble I bean."

"I didn't see your boat here earlier, Winston like the cigarettes." I said.

"Maiden voyage. Just put her in. See if she's sea worthy. There's another riff." He strummed. "We got to see if she's sea worthy, seeeeeeee—yuh!"

"Is that this house?" I asked, pointing at the painting.

"This is the house I was born in, man," he said. "Back in the day when there were proper ice caps. If she holds here for a week, I'm putting her in the Gulf."

"Seems kind of shaky."

"Don't underestimate this house," he said. "It got mad floats."

He passed me a cup of whiskey, and I told him that I don't drink anymore.

"What?" he said. "What do you use as your excuse for being an asshole then?"

"I don't have an excuse," I said.

"All right. What else? A game?" He took an orange box from the floor behind him that said Pig Mania. He rolled two plastic pigs across the table like dice. One of them landed on its back with its feet in the air. "Razorback," he said. "Ten points." He tossed a pad of paper and a pen at me. I drew two columns. One labeled *W* for him and one labeled *M* for me. On my first throw I scored a leaning jowler and I was hooked. We must have played for hours, landing the pigs in every possible configuration: sider, hoofer, snouter, double this, double that, mixed combo, making bacon...

When Winston reached for his guitar again, I walked outside and stood on the fifty-gallon drums. I felt good. I had come back to a place that was by now completely alien to me and I kind of already had two new friends. It was still mostly dark but the clouds were pink. Winston sang inside. His songs represented everything that I hated about music.

I was looking for the ladder to get back to shore when I noticed one of the dark figures leave a bench and walk across the park toward the geese. It stopped and stood for a while and the streetlight came on. Maybe I didn't see properly, but it seemed to be a girl with blonde dreads. Was it the girl? She stomped her feet and the geese startled and the streetlight went out. The geese honked.

She herded them to the side of the road. To me they were all shadows, but several of the geese seemed to walk backwards. A car turned down the street. I understood what was about to happen before it happened: the car approached, the girl lunged at the geese, the geese leapt in front of the car, the car mowed them down.

Several geese hit the windshield and flopped on the asphalt. The figure ran across the park. The geese died in the road.

I left Winston's boat and walked back to Monticello Inn room number eighteen. I fumbled for my key and opened the door. Something was not right, but it took a moment to understand it.

The table was gone. Everything else in the room was the same: Her Sheeba bike leaned against the wall, the mold in the ceiling corners, the rust marks on the pillowcases of the messed-up bed. But there was a hole in the floor where the table had been. A long tear in the carpet opened onto a dark sandy pit below. The hand towel that covered her feet hung on the frayed carpet. I turned on the lights and tried to look into the pit.

"Bregs," I shouted. My voice echoed down there. The foundation cracked slightly under my feet. I reached for the hand towel, and then I backed out slowly.

I went to the manager's office. He wore a red and blue flannel shirt. He reminded me of a comic book sketch. His hands were on the counter, like he was demonstrating that he didn't have any weapons, and there was a thin yellow ring on one of his hairy knuckles.

I put the room key on the counter.

"There's a problem in room eighteen."

"Can't do much about that."

"I didn't tell you what the problem is yet."

"Listen buddy, every room's got bedbugs. Think of them as pets. In the old days people sought out leeches, which are a lot worse than bedbugs but the same principle applies. Creature sucks blood from you. Only in one case, it's a disgusting slug-like thing and in our case it's a little and some would say even cute, not entirely unladybugish, bug. Lowers the blood pressure, especially if you drink too much."

"I don't drink."

"That's not my problem."

"A sinkhole opened up in my room. Things are missing."

"What things?"

"The table. And maybe a girl."

The man's expression changed. "What do you mean a girl?"

"I mean a girl was in the room and there's a hole and the girl is not in the room. She was asleep on the table but the table's gone."

"You checked in alone."

"I checked in alone and then I met a girl. She may be in the hole."

"You say *may be*. Who is this supposed girl fell into this supposed hole? What was her name?"

"I don't know her name. I called her Bregs. She left her bike."

"Probably she just stepped out. Let's have a look. She'll be back in a while. Or maybe she won't. You know how girls are."

He slid the key to room eighteen off the counter and I followed him out. There was a man in a hoodie leaning against the wall.

"Hey, got a smoke?" he asked.

"Sorry," I said. The manager ignored him.

"Damn, somebody got to start smoking around here," the man said.

The manager unlocked room eighteen. He looked first at the Sheeba bike. Then he looked at the hole. "Aha," he said. "I see. That's no sinkhole. Just a little floor malfunction. These things happen some times. Don't think about it. We might want to move you though."

I wheeled the Sheeba bike out, and we went back to the office. The manager handed me a key that read seventeen. "Why was she sleeping on the table?" he said. "Wait. Don't answer that."

"Should we call someone? To try and find the girl?"

"You're talking about the girl you didn't check in with whose name you don't know who you're not sure was in the room? Let's face it, buddy, we don't really know that a girl's down there, do we? What sense does it make to call someone to look for someone that we don't even know is there?"

This seemed plausible. I was still processing things. Had it been her that I saw in the park murdering geese?

I went into room seventeen. It was an exact copy of room eighteen. The same mold in the corners. The same clawed-apart bathroom door. The same rust stains on the pillow. I realized that I had forgotten my near beer in room eighteen and I no longer had a key. I went to the wall separating room seventeen from room eighteen. I pressed my ear to the floor. I smelled the sour history of thousands of feet and heard a faint *glug glug glug*.

•

The next day I rode the Sheeba bike to the beach but there was an algae bloom that washed eyeless fish onto shore and turned the air to mace. I rode back to the Monticello Inn.

From Winston's boat I watched the old ladies' funeral service for the geese. They sailed eight effigies into the lake. The effigies were approximately geese-sized paper boats. Each boat carried a wedge of flatbread. The ducks attacked the bread and sank the effigies.

The ladies' demeanor toward me changed. They were openly hostile now. And Zsa Zsa grew more vicious. When I passed, the ladies scowled at me while Zsa Zsa hissed and chased and bit my ankles. It wasn't too difficult to outrun her over a tenth of a mile, but she was remarkably quick in the short distance.

Winston's boat had proved its seaworthiness, but his friend with the truck and the winch failed to show and take him to sea. He borrowed my phone and left endless messages in a voicemail box. He kept faith. We squeezed sealant into the many gaps and spaces on deck. The boat still rocked and shifted, but he was handier and more knowledgeable than I'd first assumed. He repaired a cracked generator intake hose. He taught me how to inspect fittings.

So I just hung around there, walking nine-tenths of miles, provoking Zsa Zsa and the old ladies, tinkering with the boat, eating Styrofoams of nachos and playing Pig Mania with Winston.

When I told Winston about the sinkhole and the girl, he expressed zero surprise or concern.

"This state is a limestone sponge filled with water," he said.

"If she killed the geese then she can't be dead, right?" I said.

"Seemingly," he said, "unless it's some *Pet Sematary* kind of shit."

I hadn't thought about that movie in a long time. It had deeply affected me when I was a kid. "Winston, the last thing I heard her say was, 'See you later, alligator,' and the last thing I said to her was, 'After a while, Gomer Pyle.' She was young, man. She had no idea who Gomer Pyle was."

"Why didn't you just say 'crocodile'?"

"I don't know why I didn't just say 'crocodile.'" I worked myself into a horrific fear. "What year did *Pet Sematary* come out, Winston?"

He looked it up on my phone. "Nineteen eighty-nine," he said.

I did math. "Jesus, Winston," I said. "The girl wasn't even born yet. She wasn't even born when *Pet Sematary* came out."

At night I returned to Monticello Inn room number seventeen to wait for the girl.

A utility van was parked in front of the Monticello Inn. The side of the van read *Ground Services Inc., Providing a Solid Foundation of Trust.* The door to room number eighteen remained closed, but loud machines could be heard in there, and the earth vibrated. The sharp noises made me feel sick. For a couple days a mixing truck was backed up next to the foundation repair van.

Once I ran into a man leaving room eighteen wearing a utility belt.

"That was my room," I said.

"Bummer," he said.

"Did you find anything down there?

"A whole lot of nothing," he said.

"I had a friend who was in the room when the ground opened up. I haven't seen her since."

His expression changed. "You serious, man, or you on crack?"

"I don't do crack," I said.

He looked at me and he walked back into room number eighteen and slammed the door.

And then the utility van and the mixing truck were gone.

I went to see the manager. He looked completely different. He wore a string tie and a deerstalker hat. His lone ring was silver.

"Just the man I wanted to see," he said. "Room eighteen is ready if you're up for switching back."

"I guess I better," I said. "I like the number eighteen a lot more than seventeen."

"I wanted you to know," he said, "that we've applied a little credit to your account. For your trouble."

He slid a copy of the bill across the counter. I examined it. It looked like he knocked off around ten dollars for the week. I'd started to run out of money. The Monticello Inn wasn't much, but it added up. I considered negotiating, and then I decided not to bother. I never liked to bargain.

I wheeled the Sheeba bike from room seventeen to room eighteen. Room eighteen was dusty and had a chemical smell now. A round table identical to the one she'd slept on sat in exactly the same spot. Underneath, a large square of the carpet had been cut out and replaced with similar carpet of a slightly darker shade. My near beer was still in the mini-fridge. I reached for a can and it was hot to the touch. I pulled up a chair and sat at the table. I spread the hand towel on the table like a place mat, and I ate a Styrofoam of nachos on it. I jostled the chair. The floor was solid.

In the bathroom, the girl's zipper pouch was on the sink. I used her toothbrush.

Clearly there had been something wrong with her, I decided. She had projected someone she knew nothing about and then murdered innocent geese. I had *seen* her after all, murdering the geese. Even if that hadn't been her, if there was some dreaded geese-murderer doppleganger of her in the area that night, the odds were still good, given that she had tried to leave once already that night, she had left. She had woken up, and, while I was out in Winston's shack-boat playing Pig Mania, she left.

Then again, I thought, who knew how many nobodies like us had been swallowed up by the earth under the Monticello Inn?

I rode the Sheeba bike to the grocery store intending to get more near beer, but there was a sale on flatbread so I opted for a peace offering to Zsa Zsa and the ladies. I filled the entire front basket of the bike with flatbread and then I rode back to the lake.

It was a little early for the ladies. I sat on the bike and tore the flatbread into pieces and tossed it in the grass. The ducks and the elephantitis-head bird came to me. Eventually the remaining geese wandered over. Zsa Zsa looked suspicious. But her hiss softened. I threw her the largest pieces of bread and she snapped them up with joy. I understood that the ladies had trained the birds of the region. The avian crowd that assembled for me was a mere barn dance compared to the city of birds that the ladies attracted at their appointed daily dinner time, when the seagulls and the moorhens and the cormorants and ibises checked their schedules and flew in. I was happy with my little set though. I was surprised by the warmth I experienced feeding them. I tossed more flatbread to the stuffed animal geese. They looked completely lost without a proper flock. I felt their pain.

I had some genuine good feeling going there when the ladies appeared, giving me their dirty looks. They each carried a plastic purple chair and reusable grocery bags of bread.

"Come on, Zsa Zsa," one of them said. "Don't talk to strangers." Zsa Zsa bobbled over to her.

They set up their chairs some distance away from me. One of the ladies shouted, "We're on to you." The other told her to hush, but she didn't listen. "Everything was utopic until you and that boatman showed up. You're in cahoots with him."

"Lady, I have nothing against these birds. And me and that boatman—we're just biding our time here, same as you."

She threw a chunk of bread that narrowly missed my head. I Frisbeed a flatbread back, hitting her in the chest. She fell, and for a second I thought she might have had a heart attack. The other lady stood up, and they both shouted at me. And when they started shouting all the birds, even the normally stoic elephantitis-head bird, squawked with them.

I went the other way around the lake. *Nine-tenths of a mile, nine-tenths of a mile*, I thought. *That'll calm me down. Nine-tenths of a mile.* I hadn't run in years, but I started running, not like a jogger but like a crazy person. I'd barely make it around once before losing my breath, I figured, but the farther and faster I ran, the fuller and more deeply I breathed. And my body didn't want to stop. When I passed the old ladies they hucked more bread at me. Zsa Zsa stood at the trail's edge and snapped at my feet. I ran. I made it around again and I kept going faster and kept going faster. I soared. I flew. I saw the place for what it was, a mud puddle populated with flying rats shitting and screwing in scum. The only decent being on the lake was Winston. And there he was, giving me the thumbs up from the bow of his home, shouting "Defibrillate! Defibrillate!" I couldn't get out of breath. The lake spun by. There was Zsa Zsa barking and snapping, and I barked and snapped back. "Lunatic!" the ladies cried. "Freak!" The streetlights flashed off as I passed under them. The ladies screamed. "Goose murderer!" I was completely out of shape. But I could, if I wanted, go forever.

And then I noticed something hung on a branch near a drainpipe emptying into the lake. I stopped. The streetlight came on. I found a stick and dragged it up the bank. Her thready rasta bag, soaked and stained and smelling like dead crab. I opened it up. There wasn't much. A key ring with a single key, a white headband, a pair of mini-scissors, and several soggy packages of green tea. I scanned the lake. Had the earth spit it out over here? If so, would the table end up here as well? Her body?

I took the bag to Winston's.

"Look what I found," I said. "Look, it's hers. It means that she's dead."

"It doesn't mean anything," Winston said. "It's a purse found in a lake. Which means that it's a purse found in a lake."

Winston had some new equipment. Some kind of clear plastic bubble with a pan underneath it. He lifted the plastic bubble and turned a valve. He filled two tall, thin glasses of water and handed me one. I drank.

"A solar still," he said. "Four pints per day. Of course, ideally graphene filters, but this'll do. Desalinates seawater. It even cleans this muck." He gestured to the dark water.

"We are drinking the lake?" I said, the muscles in my stomach clenched. My insides seemed empty.

"Fresh as the sky ain't it?"

He was right. The lake water, after processing in his solar still, was fresh as the sky.

I felt my ankle where Zsa Zsa had made a bite mark the shape of a tongue depressor. Little droplets of blood raised along the outline.

We stood on the bow and night fell and the figures appeared on the benches and we listened to the things in the water around us.

"I wanted to ask you," Winston said. "Where is this Bregs you asked the girl to be?"

"I don't know."

"She's not dead is she?"

"Of course she's not dead. Why would she be dead?"

"Cause it would be kind of indelicate if you had asked that girl to be your dead old girlfriend."

"Well I asked her to be my still living ex-girlfriend. And I don't think there's anything wrong with that." But then I thought for a minute. "Come to think of it, I don't know if Bregs is dead. She could be dead I guess. I haven't seen or heard from her in eighteen years."

"It's hard finding the right people for your life," he said.

"I heard that," I said. This was something I said sometimes when I didn't know what to say.

A set of spotlights shined through the banyan tree and a horn honked.

"Winstonian!" shouted a husky voice over the rumble of bad muffler.

"Ride's here," Winston said.

It was his friend with the truck and the winch, backing down the bank toward the boat.

"This state used to be fifty percent larger ten thousand years ago," Winston said. "This right here was dry plain. Crescent Lake wasn't even a glimmer in its daddy's eye. I'm inviting you onto Winston's Ark."

"This boat is not safe, Winston," I said.

"It's all pink clouds and vultures circling here," Winston said. "It's all mouth of hell here. Your room is not safe. Out there we'll ride the wild apocalypse."

I shook Winston's hand and wished him luck. I thanked him for teaching me Pig Mania and solar water distillation. I walked across the ladder and around the lake.

The figures were again on the benches, and I decided to sit down next to one. I hung the damp rasta purse on the corner.

A man's voice said, "I know you."

"What's that?"

"I know you."

"I just moved back here, buddy. I don't know nobody."

"I know you," he said. I looked at him. And there was something familiar. It was the man in the hoodie from the hotel, the one who had asked me for a smoke.

"Oh yeah," I said. "Are you over at the Monticello too?"

"That's a bad place to stay. You got a cigarette?"

"Nope."

"Damn, for real don't nobody smoke around here."

Winston and his friend shouted instructions to each other. Their voices carried across the open space. The winch made a sound like the monkeyish scream from the banyan. Or maybe it was the monkeyish scream from the banyan and the winch was silent. I already missed Winston. I even already missed his stupid singing.

The sky was dark and the water was black and the clouds were pink again, like Winston had said. I couldn't figure out how that could be, that clouds at night were pink. And I didn't see any vultures, but that doesn't mean they weren't there.

"What that girl doing over there?" the man said and pointed across the lake.

Someone sat on the grass. From the distance it was hard to make out, but I could see that it was a girl, and in the brief interval when the streetlight was on, before, I suppose, she moved, I could see her blonde dreads. I stood up. She appeared to be throwing something at a bird, a single goose. Zsa Zsa. Even as a shadow, Zsa Zsa was unmistakable. Zsa Zsa teetered warily towards her.

If they were exactly a quarter of the way around, then it would be one fourth of nine tenths of a mile. It would take me longer to calculate the distance than to run it. I bolted, but after a few strides I gasped and heaved. My chest squeezed. When I got there my heart thumped in my eardrum, and the girl was gone. The streetlight flashed on again. I looked around.

At my feet lay Zsa Zsa's body—her neck kinked—and an empty package of flatbread. She looked dignified in death, pretty even, and I was sad that I had thought her ugly in life.

I looked at the lake: the shadows of palms stretched across the surface through the chalky reflections of the pink clouds. I shuddered.

I didn't return to the bench to pick up the rasta bag. I had a terrible sensation. I went directly back to the Monticello Inn, and I curled up on the table where the girl had slept the one night that I knew her.

But who was I kidding? I didn't know her. I didn't even try to know her. I immediately put her on Bregs and then I didn't even try to save her. I didn't bother jumping down the hole or calling the cops. What was wrong with me after all these years? I rocked the table back and forth. I stood up and rode it like a surfboard. I leapt until the leg broke and it capsized. I picked up the tabletop and smashed it against the floor. I wanted the earth to crack. I wanted the mouth of hell to open wide and swallow me up. I wanted to be down there somewhere with the real her.

VULTURES

JAQUIRA DÍAZ

ESSAY

A week after Abuela Mercy swallows five bottles of pills, as we're preparing for the funeral, my aunts Sandy and Pily bicker and yell over every arrangement, insults escalating like guerilla warfare. Each calls the other selfish, crazy, a gossip, mala, maldita hija de puta.

My mother chain-smokes outside on the steps, talking to herself.

My little cousins, Lia and Jayden, sit in their room, refusing to eat the sandwiches I brought them from Sergio's Latin Café. Who can blame them? Their grandmother has just killed herself.

Titi and her man hurl insults at each other, coming to blows, then fling shoes and hairbrushes and perfume bottles across the bedroom where my grandmother's body was found, each blaming the other for Mercy's suicide. Pily singlehandedly breaks up the fight, picks up Titi's man in a headlock, and deposits him outside the back door while we all watch. I exchange looks with my cousins Bobby and Jay. Welcome to our family.

Growing up, Bobby and Jay, my sister and I, we had an unspoken pact: as fucked up as our family was, we would not fight. The four of us, we were the normal ones. We were one force against all the crazy, the four of us against the world.

When Bobby and Jay start arguing, too, I storm out, grabbing my keys, my purse, heading to my car.

I make the four-hour drive from Miami Beach to Winter Haven alone, barreling north on US Highway 27 with the radio blasting. I'm somewhere outside South Bay when Pily calls to ask where I went.

"If you think I'm going to stay for that," I say, "you're crazy." I remind her that this is why I left Miami in the first place, that our family can't be civil, even for a funeral.

Jay calls just to tell me he loves me. Bobby calls to tell me not to feel guilty—he's not going either. When Sandy calls, she just cries on the line. After a while, I turn off my phone.

Every time I leave Miami, I tell myself I'm never coming back. I left for the Navy at eighteen, determined to stay away, see the world, see something, *anything*, only to end up right back where I started. After that, I left and came back again and again. Miami, like my family, is a place you learn to love and hate simultaneously.

When I reach Lake Okeechobee, less than halfway home, I pull into John Stretch Memorial Park on a whim, drive around aimlessly for a while, then park. All around me there is water—the park's smaller lake, the waterway that runs parallel to US 27, and then Lake Okeechobee, which spans hundreds of square miles.

In the sky, a flock of turkey vultures, bodies tilting at slight angles, wings upturned like V's. I sit on the shore of the smaller lake, watching the vultures for a long time, the pendulum swing of their bodies in the air, and wonder if they've spotted their prey, if they're waiting for something to die out here. Later, I will read that a group of vultures in flight is called a kettle, and a flock of feeding vultures, a wake.

All my life my grandmother threatened to kill herself. I visited her at the hospital when I was a kid, after she swallowed two bottles of pills and then asked Titi to call 911. I watched my uncle Junior wrestle a steak knife from her hands when she swore she would stab herself in the heart. Until she finally made good on her threats, my grandmother had been killing herself for over twenty-five years. And in some ways, taking me with her: the first time I attempted suicide I was eleven. The second time, thirteen.

On the shore, vultures circling overhead, I realize that maybe I always knew I wouldn't go to the funeral, that maybe this is where I need to be: somewhere that is not Miami, somewhere that is not Winter Haven, somewhere that is not home.

Sometimes I can't believe she did it. Sometimes, I think I always knew she would, that I've been like a bird, waiting, circling, waiting.

KIWANO

LAURA VAN DEN BERG

One summer, when I was in the tenth grade, a brain-eating amoeba killed a boy I knew. This amoeba found him when he was river swimming in Florida, not far from where my sister and I lived, and after I heard that he died, and heard how he died, I wondered if an amoeba was eating my sister's brain too, only a little at a time. I thought this because when asleep she did things like roam backyards and sidewalks; get stuck in hall closets and hedges, in doghouses and treeforts. One night, she got lost in the cool florescence of a neighbor's open freezer, where she was found eating peppermint ice cream with her bare hands.

Later my mother would say *there was no way to know*, an excuse to fall back on randomness or god or the movements of the planets instead of owning up. There are moments that foretell the future, that create an unmistakable blotch on the horizon, an eclipse—it's all there if you want to see it.

For example.

When she was fifteen, my sister sleepwalked into a 24-hour 7-Eleven. The cashier found her staring at the snack cakes—and then, he said, she disappeared. He went to call the manager and when he came back she was gone. As it turned out, she had just continued into the bathroom, where she turned on all the faucets, but when he put her name and the word "disappear" in the same sentence: the distant eclipse flared.

After the 7-Eleven incident, our parents took her to a psychiatrist, who referred her to a sleep specialist in Palm Beach, who prescribed benzodiazepine and recommended installing alarms on the windows and doors. For a while the drugs seemed like a cure, but when we were in college on opposite ends of the state—I was where Ted Bundy got his start—she confessed on the phone that she still sometimes came to on a quad or in a parking lot. "Aren't you ever afraid to go to sleep?" I asked her, and she told me no: she was only ever afraid of waking up.

Years later, in a sleep clinic in College Park, I get the feeling my own story will not end well. When the doctor appears in the examining room, the first thing I think is: she looks exactly like my sister. And then I think: no, she absolutely does not. And then I think: yes, the more I look the more she does. And then I think: stop these crazy thoughts right this minute!

Dr. Ryan is the right age and height: early thirties, five-foot-eight. Her face is a perfect oval and her eyes are storm-sky blue and her ears stick out a little. The *does so* part of my brain overlooks the slight underbite and the bump on the bridge of her nose—for who is to say my sister could not have acquired those features over time?

She introduces herself as though we've never met. The *does so* part of my brain points out that my sister could be brainwashed or have amnesia; there is no evidence to prove otherwise. Dr. Ryan is reviewing the details of my upcoming overnight, but I keep firing back with questions about where she grew up and how long has she been practicing and does she remember what she did for her twenty-fifth birthday.

"My twenty-fifth birthday?" Dr. Ryan repeats. She adjusts her glasses, my sister never wore glasses, I keep going.

"What, may I ask, is your favorite fruit?"

My sister's was the kiwano melon, which we only knew existed because our mother studied abroad in Australia. A kiwano is orange and spiked and the insides look like a jellied cucumber.

Dr. Ryan frowns. "Whatever's seasonal, I guess."

Right then it's decided: I will bring Dr. Ryan a kiwano melon and see how she responds.

I first tried to tell my husband about my sister on our fourth date, at a tapas place on Virginia Drive; in the bright space of the restaurant, I felt compelled to unspool the part of my history that blotted everything else out.

He has a right to know, I thought as little white plates arrived. A slab of toast draped with silvery anchovies that made me think of wet laundry.

Put my wife in a beautiful setting and she will ruin it with a terrible story. Later this would be one of his many grievances.

When I got to the 7-Eleven, my husband stopped me; I did not yet know him well enough to recognize his most annoying habit, the tendency to interject himself into whatever story I was trying to get out.

"My brother was a sleepwalker. He grew out of it, but when we were children he would sleepwalk into my bedroom and piss in my bed. I would wake up and find him holding his dick out like a hose."

Roasted tomatoes the size of human eyeballs appeared at our table.

"He was lucky to grow out of that," I said.

"I've never told anyone before." His face went pale and shimmery. "About my brother, I mean."

He excused himself to the bathroom and from there he sent a text, asking if I could get the bill. In the car, he apologized. He had become overwhelmed, he didn't know what was wrong. Claustrophobia maybe. He had gotten sick, he had almost passed out. He repeated the fact of having not told anyone about his brother holding his dick out like a hose.

"It was hot in there," I said. "Hot and crowded." I watched dense trees pass through the window and felt relieved that his brother lived in Texas and I would not be meeting him any time soon. I took his hand. I kissed his knuckles, one-by-one. "Just so you know, I sleep like a dead person. Soundly and lying down."

Back then I was not lying to my husband. I just missed the signs.

I am thirty-two years old and work as a program coordinator for a university chemistry department. In recent months, I have misplaced e-mails and files; rescheduled meetings I was not asked to reschedule; failed to reschedule meetings I was asked to reschedule; fallen asleep at my desk; called professors and students by the wrong name. I move like I'm pulling bags of sand behind me. I have lost thirteen pounds. There has been a minor car accident. I have mistaken a trash bag for a deer. My skin feels like cold mud.

At night, I find a window and keep watch, blood burning; the trees have mouths and are trying to tell me things. I have undergone a physical, been prescribed medications that pack my skull with cotton. With a sleep therapist, I have done paradoxical intention and biofeedback. This therapist is the one who referred me to the clinic, to better understand what is happening inside my brain.

According to my husband, during this sleepless period of my life, I have done things that are "deeply disturbing"—though I myself am in no position to judge the accuracy of this statement seeing as I have not slept normally in seventy-five days.

The clinic literature instructs me to avoid caffeine, alcohol, and naps prior to the overnight; it suggests I pack as I would for a hotel stay. The literature does not suggest I swing by the grocery and spend eight dollars on a kiwano melon; the literature does not suggest I toss the receipt on the way home and place the melon in my suitcase.

My husband and I live in a rented bungalow on Yates Street, not far from Lake Ivanhoe, and in the backyard we swat away insects in the damp, warm spring. The grass is a lush green, the air leaden from an afternoon rain.

A technician will stick sensors all over my body and these sensors are linked to wires and these wires are linked to computers. All through the night the technician will monitor my brain waves and breathing patterns and blood oxygen levels.

I read this part of the literature aloud to my husband, who wishes I was more like my parents: they planted a cherry tree in their backyard, in my sister's honor, and then decided to never speak her name again.

On the fire escape, my husband is not listening. He is interrupting. He is saying something about how our lawyer called and Mart Collins is willing to drop the petition, that he is sympathetic, given the circumstances, but he will need certain assurances from me and he will need them in writing. And then I am not listening because the kiwano melon has appeared between us. Every time my husband says "Mart Collins" the melon triples in size and soon I can't see him at all. I dig my nails into the orange flesh. Between two thorns I carve an opening and crawl inside and wait to be suffocated by the green guts, but, to my surprise, I find that I am able to breathe.

Here is the part you have been waiting for.

The twenty-fifth birthday. The weekend in Daytona Beach. Has anything good ever come from a weekend in Daytona Beach? The hotel room on the thirteenth floor. From the window I could see golden sand; the rippling tide; a boardwalk.

We got pedicures and sunburns. We ate shrimp cocktails in bed, swaddled in plush bathrobes. Our official drink was the Dark and Stormy.

On the third night, I woke to find her covers turned back, her body gone. Later, on a grainy security video screen, I would watch her sleepwalking down the hallway, in a pair of unlaced sneakers, and knocking on doors—and I swear I knew what was going to happen before it did. A door would open. She would vanish into room 1315, occupied by one Mart Collins. The door would close. I would never see her again.

.

If my parents had foreseen the blotch on the horizon of her life, I wonder what they would have been willing to do. Have her institutionalized; frame her for a terrible crime so she gets life in jail; hire a chaperone who never sleeps; lock her away in a tower, like a princess in a fairytale; arrange for her to be put into a coma. In the middle of the night, any of these options seem reasonable to me.

Charlemagne was her favorite king. Quadratic equations is her favorite math. For the last five years, neither tense has sounded right.

After thirteen minutes in Mart Collins's room, they drove in his truck to an IHOP. This was also documented by security cameras and eyewitnesses eating pancakes. In his statement, Mart Collins said my sister just wanted to talk, he never touched her. At the IHOP, she ordered Double Blueberry Pancakes before disappearing into the bathroom, like she did in the 7-Eleven, only this time she never came back. He says her last words were, "I'll have a Double Blueberry, please."

The "please" always stops me. It is unlike my sister to have said "please."

In the end, the police concluded Mart Collins was not guilty of a crime and, not long after, the investigation went cold. A sister never goes cold. After 23 days of not sleeping, I tracked Mart Collins down online. I started with the e-mails and the calls, to his office and then to his home. I left messages, I mailed letters, I mailed photos of my sister as a child.

All those hours in the night, I had to find a way to fill them.

In his statement, Mart Collins said it was hard to be a good person and being a good person can land you in trouble just as readily as being a bad person, as evidenced by his presence in an interrogation room. Yet my sister seemed troubled and he could not help but show kindness to strangers in need. That was his excuse for taking her to IHOP at three in the morning. Anyone who gives a statement like that has to be guilty of something.

In the clinic waiting room, I notice a chart like the ones in optometrist offices, but instead of letters there are eyeballs of varying size, pulsing in the manner of anguished cartoon characters. I recall a TV program about a murder in Scranton: every night at four-thirty in the morning a mother heard the voice of her daughter, saying *postmark postmark postmark*. The woman's daughter had been murdered six months ago, her estimated time of death was four-thirty in the morning, and when the police finally investigated their mailman? Body parts in his freezer.

I wait for my name to be called.

In the examining room, the nurse recording my vitals informs me that I am not scheduled to see Dr. Ryan again until the results of my sleep study have come back.

"But I need to see her today." I picture handing the kiwano melon to Dr. Ryan, her hands closing around it like nightfall, the cloud of recognition crossing her face: *I am holding a thing I used to love*. "I have a gift for her."

"You'll make your next appointment at check-out. You can leave your gift with the receptionist." A stethoscope is looped around her neck; she holds the chestpiece in her palm. "Anyway Dr. Ryan is not in the office today."

Later, in a hallway, I pass the door with Dr. Ryan's name on it, letters etched across a little airstrip of brass.

When I learned Mart Collins had moved to Port Charlotte the next step was obvious. On day 61 of not sleeping, I drove away from College Park at dawn; my plan was to intercept him before he left for work. As I neared his house, I imagined finding my sister inside. All this time she had been alive and happy, just over 100 miles away. They had fallen in love, her and Mart. They had run away together because they knew their families wouldn't approve—Wait, why wouldn't we have approved?

This scenario was interrupted when a young women answered the door. She was wearing black track pants and a sweatshirt, her hair pushed back from her forehead by a cloth headband. Apparently Mart Collins, who had recently broken his hip in a skiing accident, had a daughter.

"He's on painkillers," the daughter said. "He's asleep."

"I'm a friend," I said. "I heard about his accident. I'm here to visit. To help."

"A friend from where?"

"From Chicago." This was where Mart Collins was living when my sister disappeared.

"If you live in Chicago, what are you doing here?"

"We met on vacation," I said. "In Daytona Beach. Before he moved here."

A mistake. Her chest began to heave a little.

She slammed the door so hard the air vibrated. I lingered on the lawn and after we made eye contact through a downstairs window she ran around closing all the curtains and blinds. I watched the house go dark, one window at a time.

On the last leg home, near Sebring, I somehow drove into a telephone pole. In the Emergency Room, my husband wanted to know if I was afraid. He started rubbing my neck and though I knew his hand was on my skin, could picture his fingers counting vertebra, I couldn't feel a thing. *You can't let this define you*, he said, and it took all the love I had to not punch him in the face.

The clinic literature describes the rooms as comparable to hotel rooms, not inaccurate if the rooms in question are intended to resemble the worst of their kind. The walls are the color of a rancid pond, the bedspread itchy and mauve. There is no clock. A tiny black TV is mounted in the corner. The bed faces a one-way mirror and I think immediately of *Law & Order*.

The technician leaves me alone to change. I put on sweatpants and thick socks and a t-shirt with the slogan IF YOU'RE NOT PART OF

THE SOLUTION YOU'RE PART OF THE PRECIPITATION, a gift from the chemistry department. The melon was wrapped in this t-shirt, so now it sits naked between my toiletries bag and sneakers. I push the suitcase under the bed.

My sister used to say sleepwalking felt like splashing around in a warm bath.

The technician returns holding an armful of white wires, clips and sensors dangling from the tips. "Time to get comfortable," he says.

He sticks sensors to my temple, scalp, torso. He fastens elastic belts around my chest and belly. White clips hang like earring from my ears. Another clip on my left index finger. The sensors are cold. They make me want to scratch until I see blood. The wires connect me to a cluster of standing monitors, like a person hooked up to life support.

I watch TV until lights out. Lo and Behold, *Law & Order* is on, and I remember my sister standing on her bed in Daytona Beach and reciting lines from Jack McCoy's best closing arguments. *Where does that other eighteen thousand dollars go? To your Jaguar, your summer home, that fifteen hundred dollar suit you're wearing now?*

There is one moment about that night I have never discussed with anyone—and try to avoid discussing with myself. How I woke at two-thirty in the morning and found her bed empty. How I glimpsed the closed bathroom door and the sheet of light on the carpet and felt my heart still: she was just using the bathroom, like anyone else's sister. How my brain was fogged with the last good night's sleep I would ever have and too many Dark and Stormys. How I did not open the door and make sure she was there.

In the clinic, in the dark of my room, I can't stop thinking about the kiwano melon and how it must be getting worried. The *does so* part of my brain reminds me of the office nameplate and how Dr. Ryan looked like a hard worker, a workaholic even—she could have snuck back to her office under the cover of night; she could be hunched under a desk lamp, examining files.

I press a button. The technician appears. I say I need the bathroom. He sighs and disconnects me from the machines. The clips snap as they slide off my ears. *Already?* I can tell he's thinking. He says he'll wait in the room.

"I might be a while," I say, and he leaves without another word.

In the hallway, as I make my escape, I hear two voices and at first I think it's the *does so* and *does not* sides of my brain, arguing again, but one voice sounds like my own and the other sounds different—and then I realize it's my sister, speaking from an invisible place.

You haven't slept in months, I try to tell myself, you're losing your grip. Shadows move like eels across the ceiling. I press the melon against my chest. *I am responsible*, I say, and my sister tells me, *No, there were other forces at work.*

Briefly, a third voice: the technician chasing after me.

Then my sister drowns everything out.

A missing person can be anywhere, at any time. She could be Dr. Ryan or the homeless woman on the roadside or chained up in that passing van or rotting in a landfill or living in a convent, her sleepwalking cured by prayer. At any moment it is theoretically possible I will bump into her on the street, though it is also theoretically possible extensive plastic surgery has been performed, making her unrecognizable to me. The problem is not the absence of answers, but that there are too many answers—and no clear way to even begin.

I believe in all the answers, except the most obvious one.

Doors fly open. Night pricks my arms. My sister is telling me to forget Dr. Ryan, she is not who I want her to be. The kiwano melon is for Mart Collins, it is for bashing him in the face, and right then I understand I'm holding *two* things in my hands: the melon and my car keys.

I could drive to Port Charlotte and not stop for anything.

In the parking lot, I put the melon on the roof of the car and for a moment, I am seized by a terrible thought: I am going to run this melon the fuck over.

Not yet, my sister says.

I need a minute, I need to breathe, but my sister is saying *go*.

I look down.

Sneakers on, laces undone. How did they get there? The eclipse flares, and a near-future self says, *I couldn't have done what you say. I don't even know how my shoes got on my feet.*

THE LAMPSHADE

ASHA DORE

ESSAY

When the television told us a storm was coming, we filled the bathtubs with water and checked the flashlight batteries. We set matches and candles on the kitchen counter. We gathered pecans from the grass in the backyard and stripped the fruit trees, carrying kumquats and key limes into the house in blue plastic Easter baskets. We almost never needed to buy extra canned goods. Hurricanes threatened and sometimes hit a couple times a year, so we kept our pantry stocked.

At some point during the storm, right before the eye, the wind knocked out the power. Lights dark, TV dark, the dogs whining. Mom asked, "What's in the pantry?" I sat on the floor with a marker, a flashlight, and a notebook. I made a list. Here's what we have, and here's how long we can live on it. When the eye spread out over the town, my brother and I went outside. "How does it feel to walk around inside an eye?" Dad asked. We shrugged and spread out a blanket on the front lawn. Everything went still. No rain, a little wind, debris tumbling slowly down the sidewalks. Above us, the clouds sped past.

When I was fifteen, Dad died. During the months leading up to his death, toxins from his failing liver threaded through his body and brain. Some afternoons, he walked up to me like he wanted to ask a question but stopped, started a syllable, looked up at the ceiling, rolled his eyes, and sighed. Instead of searching again for his words, he picked up his guitar from its station beside the fireplace. He sat on his denim recliner, picking at chords until he fell asleep.

When I was five years old, Dad opened a business selling fire alarms. He and Mom drove to grocery stores in Northwest Florida and set up cardboard drop-boxes. They glued a small pad of paper and a pen with a long, coiled cord to the side of each box. Behind the boxes, they put up signs made out of red, hand-cut letters on white poster board: *Win a $100 Gift Certificate!*

The small print: *To be eligible for the Grand Prize, please include your full name, address, and phone number. Your name and all other identifying information will also be included in a raffle for additional prizes presented by MasterGuard of Northwest Florida in affiliation with Ryan's Steakhouse, Cock of the Walk, Joe Patti's Seafood and Café, and the Fish House, True Value, Home Depot, Jerry's Diner, the City of Pensacola, Pensacola Beach, Navarre, Cantonment, and Destin.*

On Saturdays, Mom and I stopped by to empty the boxes. I held open a trash bag. Mom pulled open the serrated cardboard flap on the back of the box and dumped a couple dozen squares of paper into the trash bag. The squares of paper were called *leads*. At home, we dumped out the bag, opened up a map of Pensacola, and sorted the leads by region. North Hill, East Hill, Bayfront, West side. I made a separate list for each stack, names and phone numbers.

Before I turned ten, I sat beside Mom while she called each number on the list. "Hello, I'm Stephanie from MasterGuard of Northwest Florida," she said. "Do you remember putting your name in a box to win a $100 gift certificate? I'm sorry to say, you weren't one of the grand prize winners, but you are eligible for a free fish dinner at Ryan's for you and your spouse. How does that sound?"

When they answered, if Mom nodded, I circled their name with a pink marker. If Mom shook her head, I crossed out their name with a black pen. I listened as Mom scheduled four to five couples per night for dinner and a quick presentation. Those nights, I sat on the floor in the corner of the dining room at Ryan's Steakhouse while couples shuffled into the back room. I drew horses and long, green pastures while Dad played a video about burned houses and smoke inhalation. Under the light from images of curtains catching fire, I colored in a bright orange cloud. I listened to the recorded voices of burn survivors while I dotted the grass on my drawing with pecans. I listened to the servers sliding plates of steaming fish and greens and cornbread in front of the couples, my body curled around my page, drawing the fine details: the horses' eyelashes, their nostrils, the bows in their manes.

Dad walked from table to table, cupping his fire alarm in the crook of his elbow. He told the couples how fast a flame eats through a family. He nodded in my direction. The couples followed his eyes. I pretended to color the grass again, my wrist loose, my face hot. "Before she was born," he said, "I wasn't afraid of anything."

He told them about the lamp on my bedside table, the lampshade that someone knocked a little sideways one day, without noticing. He told them I was maybe two years old when I fell asleep with that lamp on. He told them that I woke up crying, swatting at the bulb, the lampshade melted around it, a small flame. He told them that he and Mom had just fallen asleep when I woke up crying, and they turned in bed, telling each other I'd fall asleep any second, telling each other, "Just wait." He told them he'd had to piss anyway, so he decided to get up and check. He talked about it like it was some magic that he found me right before the wall or my skin caught the flame. He didn't tell them that he really got up to search for whiskey. He didn't repeat the refrain he'd delivered to Mom throughout my childhood: "That damn whiskey saved our daughter's life."

Standing in the restaurant, Dad held his fire alarm tight against his chest. He looked at the couple, their forks half stuck in a filet of red snapper. "We're still here," he said. "And so are you."

The sales pitch.

The hot fear that will follow me around for the rest of my life.

A fire lurking in something hidden. A frayed wire. A toaster oven left plugged in overnight. A battery in the laundry room lint basket. When I go to bed at night, I list the dangers, the things that could catch fire and eat through my family. I wake up in the middle of the night, walk through the quiet dark checking for sparks and smoke. "It's not a matter of *if*," Dad would say, "but *when*."

After Dad died, I went through his closet, hoping to find souvenirs from his life before me, or at least money. Maybe he was a secret collector of wild animal teeth or seashells. Maybe I'd find a stack of foreign bills or coins from his travels in South America. Maybe a protest sign from the Vietnam War or a sign he held while hitchhiking up the West Coast or even a notepad filled with to-do lists, notes to self, a diary. I dug through his pants pockets and found worry stones and lint. I pulled out each pair of his underwear, folding them into a trash bag, one at a time. Underneath, the drawer was empty. I dug through his shoes, his coat sleeves, the junk drawer in the kitchen. I found appliance manuals, paid bills, receipts, batteries, half-dried sticks of glue. In his office, I found a drawer filled with used grocery store leads held together with rubber bands. I found clipboards filled with lists, strangers' names, telephone numbers, some of them circled with pink marker, some of them crossed out. I stood in the pantry door, logging the items that had been left behind.

flour
sugar
peaches
water chestnuts
chicken and stars
baby corn

I couldn't make much of a meal, but, as usual, there was something to eat. On the shelf at the top of the pantry, I found a cigar box filled with pieces of paper folded into tiny squares and underneath them, a plastic sandwich bag filled with baby teeth.

I realized later that everything I found in Dad's house was a souvenir of his life since me. I considered the possibility that Dad wasn't bullshitting the couples at the Free Steak Dinners. Maybe he believed his somewhat distorted, rock-bottom-to-riches version of the American Dream: he had to almost lose his kid to realize he wanted a family. He had to find fear first, and once he wanted us, that feeling stayed.

Most of the items I found at Dad's house were thrown away, sold at a yard sale, or grabbed up by one of the cousins, but I remember them, the catalog of the first fifteen years of my life, the ingredients necessary to make a nuclear family, a family blooming up from the fear, right on the edge of burning.

On the night he went unconscious, nineteen hours before the surgical resident pulled the intubation from his throat and turned off his machines, Dad forgot my name. He sat up on the chrome bed in the hallway of the emergency room. "Nurse," he said to me. "Where are my kids?"

"They're safe," I said. I nodded toward my brother who sat on a white plastic chair in the waiting room, playing his handheld SEGA.

Dad followed my gaze and relaxed a little. He narrowed his eyes at me. "Nurse," he said. "Why aren't you wearing a name dog.

"I mean turt...turtle.

"I mean tag.

"I mean, where is your name?"

The names went first, then his body, a slow death. Before him, most of his family had died fast. His dad from emphysema complicated by some kind of infection, his sister from a heart attack in her early thirties, one sister-in-law from suicide and one from cancer, and his nephew from asphyxiation after too much booze. All of them lived in North Florida or Southern Alabama most of their lives, sucking down weed and coke and alcohol, waiting for the hot Gulf water to carry the storms across their houses and bodies, waiting for the rain to flood them out or the wind to knock off their roofs, their screen doors, the side panels on their mobile homes and trailers. They waited, knowing that tornadoes could drop down through their kitchen ceilings, knowing sinkholes could open underneath their bedrooms, their living rooms, swallowing the furniture and the bedside table and the shoes they kicked off when they walked in the door. They stayed, like everyone else in Pensacola, like my Dad's customers, knowing that a storm was coming.

They weren't worried about the storms. Or the floods. Or the drowning. They filled out little squares of paper, hoping to win a $100 grocery store shopping spree. They ate their free steak and fish and cornbread. They filled up their credit cards buying smoke detectors and heat alarms. They worried about fire.

I'm pretty sure nobody ever won a $100 gift certificate, but about a hundred families a year let Dad into their homes to install a constellation of metal orbs against their ceilings. Smoke detectors dotted the halls of their houses. Heat alarms flickered from the ceilings of kitchens and garages. A carbon monoxide alarm had been drilled into every bedroom. All of them blinking orange or yellow or green. A silent orchestra of small lights putting a whole coast of families to sleep.

In our house, I carried my fire alarm like it was a sleeping cat, hands cupped around the cool edges, feet stepping on the cold wood floor. The alarm was a beige, flat circle—heavy, so I had to hold it with two hands. I lifted it up to Dad where he stood on a ladder in our living room. He leaned down to grab it with just one hand. Pulled his screwdriver from between his teeth. Pressed the alarm into the ceiling. Pushed a screw through the metal holes on the edges.

Dad read Stephen King novels while he drove from house to house to house to sell alarms. Read one line, look at the road, read a line, look at the road, line, road, line, road. That's how Dad taught me to drive on the interstate. "It keeps you safe and alive," he'd tell me. "It keeps you awake."

When I'm on the road, I take his advice. I make lists of things to do and things to buy and meals to cook for dinner. I fill my brain up with plans, with nouns, with names. I stay awake, driving, preparing, still alive.

The year Dad died, a hurricane was supposed to hit, but then it didn't. The pecans from the backyard tree should have been blown all over the neighborhood, but they weren't. The hurricane's eye faded out or turned just enough to pass my hometown, to flatten some other house, some other family.

The day before Dad died, he had been doing better. Less confused. More awake. Talking about giving everything away and moving out west. A new start, a new life, somewhere else. When I walked into Dad's house the night before he died, the lights were off, and I thought he must be asleep. I lay on the couch, thankful he didn't catch me missing curfew, but then it came, my name. In the back hallway, I found Dad shuffling slowly through the dark. I was one third of Dad's size, but I tried to carry him anyway. My brother woke up and wrapped Dad's arm around his shoulder. Half bent under the weight of him, we moved to the car. On the drive, I don't remember if there were words, but I remember a thunderstorm was flooding the city. I remember the water spilling across the road on the way to the hospital. I remember thinking about how random thunderstorms did more damage than hurricanes most of the time, but we did almost nothing to prepare for them. No county evacuations or gouged gas prices or driving advisories. Most of the time, the boys from my high school went out to surf during those nameless storms, some of them wrecking their bodies, some of them drowning.

Right before we arrived at the hospital, the rain stopped. My brother and I helped Dad step over a metal drain in the middle of the parking lot, the sound of water rushing below us. In the waiting room while my brother played SEGA, I imagined the trip out west Dad had been talking about. The long, dry drive through Texas. The gloss of the sun there, less humidity, I imagined. Desert tropical. A paradise on the other side of the country, mirror image of Florida, all citrus and palm trees without the snakes and sinkholes and hot wet pressure and storms. "A place like that," Dad had said, "barely seems possible. But it is. I've been there, a long time ago, and it is."

On family vacations, Dad sat in the driver's seat telling stories about his life. He said, "Before you were born, I was a pirate." When he said "pirate," he meant "drug runner." He meant that he smuggled in barrels of weed and narcotics through the port of New Orleans. Dad told me, "After you were born, I wanted to help people." I think he meant: instead of hurting them. Instead of delivering addiction to new bodies, he wanted to protect them. Maybe he wanted to even out all the bad. Maybe he wanted to make enough money to protect our family, to help us crawl out of his history, the parts of his story that he left out. Maybe a little bit of both.

I still can't decide if the fire alarm company was legitimate or a total scam, but after Dad died and after the power had been turned off at his house, I went back. The sunrise was all pink and orange clouds, broken up with lines of pale blue. Dad's closet was lit by the gold of that light, getting darker. I dug through his things, again, still searching for something. Shoved in the back, behind his shoes, I found a box filled with newspaper clippings. House fires in Northwest Florida. Families standing in a line, smiling below headlines. Families with Dad's alarms installed in their blackened ceilings. Families who didn't die or burn. Families saved.

A year before I was born, my mom met my dad through her drug dealer. Mom knew Dad drank and did coke, like her, but she didn't know that he had been infected with Hepatitis C at least a decade before, likely during the years he lived in San Francisco and intermittently used and sold heroin. When I was conceived, they both quit using for a while. Dad started drinking again around my second birthday. The more he drank, the more my parents fought, until the lampshade caught fire. Dad quit drinking, again. He found the fire alarm company, started selling, opened a franchise, and told me at least a few times a year just how many times I had accidentally saved his life.

The night I drove Dad to the hospital, I thought, here it is again, another story of me and Dad, one way or another bringing our family out of whatever darkness and into the next phase of our lives. This time, it would be moving out West, and this time, unlike all the other times, I was old enough to remember it. I had prepared for a night like this. Packed a hospital bag filled with a change of clothes and soap and toothpaste and a list of questions to ask the doctors. Snuck an extra pair of Dad's flip-flops onto the floor in front of the passenger seat, in case he was too stubborn or too sick to slip on his loafers. Kept the gas tank full and snacks in the glove box.

I hadn't learned yet that you can't save someone on purpose. You can't plan for anything but the leftovers, and even then, there are questions, like, What happens when you lose your family for the same reason you got them in the first place? A charred liver or a charred wall. The good cancelled out by the bad or the other way around.

The "what if" of it is completely useless, but still, the elements stack up. Flour, sugar, yeast, baby corn, chicken soup, salt, no weed and no coke, no mobile homes, no hurricanes, no fire alarms, no lampshade, no whiskey. If there were no whiskey, there'd be no daughter either. Maybe just a nurse standing there beside his hospital bed. Her grey eyes under the fluorescent lights instead of mine would be his last stillness before the toxins from his liver put him to sleep. I can imagine the way his forearm feels when she touches it right before he goes unconscious, the skin tight around the edema, his body retaining water as it breaks down. I can imagine it, but the nurse, she barely notices. She watches his eyes close, his fists unclench, his neck relax, and she moves on to the next patient, the next person on the edge of something. She touches their forearm, too. She takes their pulse. She listens to their breathing until they disappear.

RIGHTNESS

JOHN HENRY FLEMING

FICTION

I was on my way to the baseball game to sell my ticket. The Rays were playing the Dodgers. When I bought the ticket last week, I thought it would be a good game, two average teams fighting to prove they were slightly better than average. But I needed the money, so I decided to sell. I shouldn't have bought the ticket in the first place. I'd maxed out my last credit card, and I'd never have money to make the payment. The card would get canceled like the others, and it would be a long time before I could get another card. Those are some thoughts I would have had if I'd done the due diligence in my head. But when it comes to knowing things, there's also something like a seawall that blocks certain facts when they break on your shore. For me the seawall was a feeling, a hope that things could change. And when you have that hope, you don't feel the need to think through the odds of things like windfall money, you're just aware that some people come into it, so why not you? In fact, it's better not to get into details because if you do—if you think about specific people giving you certain amounts of money for particular reasons—those thoughts are like cracks in your seawall, and then it doesn't take much for the waves to blast through. Anyway, if you're living without hope, you're not really living, right?

The Rays-Dodgers game was for me a symbol of hope, a dove shook from a cage and flying up into the rainbows or whatever, except that's overstating it, really. The game gave me something to look forward to, is all I mean, and that was enough. I didn't need doves or rainbows to complete the picture, though now that I think about it, in the days leading up to the game I did sometimes imagine a home-run ball arcing like a rainbow into left field, my seat being on the first base line, a pretty good one, and my imagination picturing the scene from that position, watching the ball from a Rays slugger sail through the dome at the Trop while everyone jumps up and cheers and there's a kind of community moment, which is about as close as you're going to get to an indoor rainbow.

What I'm saying is that I let my defense down. I had to sell the ticket, and that put me in a bad mood, a hopeless mood, and that's pretty much what led to the incident, including all the blood and the guy dying on the side of the road.

I wish it hadn't happened. I could blame a lot of things, but mostly I can blame myself, even ignoring the fact that I swung a baseball bat at the guy's head, because even before that there's the fact that I got the ticket in the first place when I shouldn't have, and the fact that I decided to cash it in and buy a little weed to smoke while I watched the game at home, because I'd realized I could buy the weed, smoke, and watch, and still have a few bucks left over for food, where if I went to the game I wouldn't even have the money for a hot dog, even with it being two-dollar dog night. For a certain kind of person, those are reasonable thoughts. For a certain kind of person, the wisdom of staying home and settling for less creates another kind of hope, where the settling is a kernel for personal growth, financially or whatever. I'm not that kind of person. I'm the kind of person who knows for sure that he really has no hope, knows it and can't admit it, and so he sometimes impersonates a person with hope, disappointing himself every time. Because the next day I'll be back to my job digging fiber optic trenches so the kinds of people I'm not can get high-speed internet, or I'm checking in with my probation officer, or I'm looking for some way to replace the battery in my car because these days I have to find someone to jump it every time I need to use it, which is the kind of thing that makes my neighbors and friends leave early for work, not even because they don't want to help me but more likely because I don't know how to ask a favor like a regular person, especially after about the tenth time, so I have to either make up some obviously bogus reason they owe me a favor or act like a pathetic fuckup who doesn't really care. I'm that kind of person.

I'm not making excuses. Even before all that, there's the way I got myself into this situation in the first place, having mouthed off to the course superintendent one too many times at my last job when after all it was my fault for staying out late and coming to work still pretty buzzed from all the tequila and cigars and ignoring that I had the kind of job where I had to get up at 5:30 and start work at dawn before the golfers showed up, where I had to operate machinery to get the greens and fairways and rough mowed, or the new trees watered, or the weeds killed or the pipes dug up for the irrigation man to fix, a job that maybe I should have had more respect for, knowing as I do now that losing it would mean I'd be digging ditches for daily work and half pay and falling behind on every bill and generally feeling hopeless about everything. I'd pretended to be too good for that job—another bad case of the hopes—and acted like I could spend all my money on tequila and cigars and still have plenty left for the usual things people survive on, all the while copping the attitude that I'd really only been a step or two away from an office job if I'd just listened to the people who said I was smart and stayed in school all the way through, in which case I'd now be sleeping in every day and the late-night tequila wouldn't take the same toll, because no one really cares or notices if you're wobbly drunk in an office because you can talk drunk and sell things drunk and if you're good at drinking and selling no one will care.

I made mistakes. I maybe had a smaller margin for error than those people with fiber optic internet, but I admit I covered the spread. Why would I even keep a bat in the car in the first place? Did I think I was still going to make it as a baseball player? Did I think my old high school coach would come and beg me back on the team after I spit in his face ten years ago?

I'm not stupid. I know myself. The bat was in there because it was part of who I am, or who I think of myself as, or who I still wish I could be, or wish I could still wish. The bat had been rolling around the floor of my back seat for years. Did I ever imagine using it on someone's head? I did. I thought of it. I'd never picked it up with that intention before, but sometimes when I heard it back there, or caught sight of the handle sticking out of the Whopper wrappers and Coke cans on the floor, I thought how I could just grab it and swing it at someone—particularly someone who lived life like he could ignore that possibility—and how I was uniquely qualified for swinging it, having hit .480 and twenty-seven home runs in my junior year and getting looked at even then by scouts, and just think about how many people keep bats by their doors or even, like me, in their cars, and fantasize about living out a movie scene, when the truth is that they probably wouldn't have the guts to swing the bat in the heat of the moment, or else wouldn't have the skill to swing it with accuracy or with the kind of power you need to knock someone down and make sure they won't get back up and shoot you or stab you. As for me, my thought was that if anyone deserved to have a bat and deserved to use it in a situation, it was me.

So I'd given myself the green light years before, and even though I didn't really think about it, the green light was there, and when the appropriate situation arose, I acted without a mental debate, which might have saved my life if the guy had had a gun, or could at least have seemed justified if the guy *looked* like he might have a gun, but the guy didn't have a gun or anything resembling it, so I never felt threatened by anything worse than the look on his face.

I could blame myself for feeling threatened if the other reasons didn't make me guilty enough already. Really, how many reasons do you need? You kill a person with a baseball bat, and that should be enough. You don't accidentally swing a baseball bat, not the way I did. You don't accidentally destroy someone's jaw and crush half his skull. I'm guilty. In all ways guilty.

It will turn up in the newspapers as a "road rage incident." I've read plenty of reports like that. I've seen them on the TV news and on YouTube. Someone cuts someone off, someone gets pissed, and pretty soon the words turn to violence. If there's a gun around, it gets used. A knife, used. A baseball bat, used, probably. And then, reading the story, you have to wonder about the people. You feel sorry for the victim and the victim's family, and you hate the guts of the perpetrator, but it's the perpetrator you think about most. What kind of person does that? What kind of person lets a moment's rage turn him into a killer? How long had he been simmering? How long walking among the rest of us, locked and loaded? How many others just like him?

I was on the highway, speeding, not too much. Keeping up with the speeders. Found myself blocked by a left lane hog. Man or woman, black, white, Hispanic, I don't know. You tend to look over when you drive around people like that. You try to keep a tally in your head. Who's the most likely to drive slow in the fast lane? Who's talking on the phone or texting? Who's wasted? You keep a tally so you can sort out the people. I don't know why. The information's never going to come in handy. If left lane hogs are most likely to be Hispanic women talking to their boyfriends, what difference does it make? Still, you want to know. You want to have a shorthand way of judging. I didn't look through the passenger window of the lane hog and add to one or the other's tally because, as I moved into the middle lane, someone else was moving in at the same time from the outside lane. We bumped fenders and swerved, almost involved two or three other vehicles, but no, just us.

We both pulled over. Things escalated, as they say in the reports.

The side of the highway is the worst place for a disagreement. We were in the late stages of rush hour. Dense traffic moving fast. The cars making big sighs as they pass. Trucks like giant fists just missing your face. The road shoulder's not big, and you're kind of squeezed onto a strip where someone's tweet could take you out. The asphalt's releasing a day's worth of summer heat. The sick soup of humidity and fumes fills your lungs. A pair of cars with dings and, if there's any insurance, it's going up or getting canceled. Two drivers feeling wronged. I'm not making excuses.

There was this moment when everything could have gone differently. Not anything like one of those quiet moments you see in the movies, not with all the traffic. We both opened our driver's doors. Both looking forward to expressing our righteous indignation.

The other guy was a black guy. I should say that now. But it was obvious the guy was a lot like me. He drove a piece of shit car. He dressed like he had no money and gave up a long time ago trying to pretend. All he had left were brief psychic holidays of self-deception when he could muster them up, and even that was getting hard. Really, the fender bender was a gift. Forget about the cost. For once, he was totally sure he was right about something, and he was going to have the pleasure of expressing his rightness to whatever extent he saw fit, because when hope dries up, you take rightness over nothing. This guy was just like me, which meant that only one of us could be right.

Seeing the exact same look on the other guy's face only made me angrier. The look was a challenge to my rightness. He was trying to wrestle it away from me, and the only way to get it back was to out-anger him. I could see he felt the same way. The time for one of us to back down had already passed. It had passed when we stepped out of our cars and realized we were the same. It's like in the card game War; when two players turn over the same card, there's a war. It's that simple; it's the rules. The only thing that might have stopped us was if we didn't know the rules. But the rules are the sort of thing you know whether you've played the game before or not. The rules are part of living.

He charged first. That's not an excuse. He saw my look, and he got offended just like me, and his righteous anger took the form of lowering his head and charging at me. Mine took the form of reaching into my car and grabbing the baseball bat. I got the bat when I was sixteen, a Mizuno Nighthawk. I'd hit twenty-seven junior-year home runs with it. I liked the ring of the aluminum bell when I made solid contact. I liked the vibration running through my palms and up my arms into my shoulders, the powerful metallic wobble. The guy should have seen I'd use it. I think he did, and didn't care. When I swung, he didn't even put up his arms, not that there was much time. The scouts said I had good bat speed, and I hadn't lost much in the years since. Either the guy didn't care or he put up his own seawall to block the facts. When was the last time he'd felt so clearly in the right? When was the last time he'd had the opportunity to prove it? It gave him his hope back. Anyway, unexpected things do sometimes happen. Maybe I'd back down. Maybe I'd miss. Maybe the bat would break or slip out of my hand. Of course he knew these things weren't going to happen, but a little moment of hope was worth the consequences, so he put up a seawall to feel safe and hopeful in his very last moments, and in his mind it was worth it.

It had been a while, but I still knew how to swing a bat. I uncoiled. I stepped into it and snapped my wrists. He didn't try to get out of the way.

I smashed in the left side of his face and felt the vibration of his cracking skull all the way up into my shoulders.

He was dead before he hit the ground.

I dropped the bat. Traffic slowed. Someone honked a horn. I stood there on the shoulder. Meanwhile, the guy's blood was leaking out of his head. His jaw was a mess I didn't want to look at. I want to say there was something pretty about the sky, but it wasn't sunset yet. It was the kind of sky you'd expect at the end of rush hour. Hazy and graying into dusk. In a few minutes, I was going to get arrested, go to trial, and spend the rest of my life in prison, but for a moment I was still right there, watching the ball arc over the outfield, just possibly on its way out of the park.

LIGHTNING: AN ESSAY IN FLASHES

AMY PARKER

he Skeletons of Girls
When I was little, I was afraid of lightning because I thought it was the flash of God's Polaroid camera going off. Adults reminded me—even Bette Midler on the radio reminded me—that God is watching us. That includes me. All. The. Time. When I'm taking my clothes off before a shower. When I get dressed. When my head sways to music. When I'm eating too many peanut butter cookies. When I hit my younger brother. When I'm going to the bathroom.

Does God edit out anything, turn His eyes away for a second to see what others are up to?

I guess I thought God was a multi-eyed creature with lots of cameras all over the world.

But a lot of the flashes took place around me. He needed evidence that I wasn't as good as I claimed I was. As I pretended I to be.

In college, I wrote an essay in which I used lightning as a metaphor for electroconvulsive therapy (ECT). I was in the middle of the storm back then, unable to see outward through the thick. During the summer of 2006, I had had 10 treatments of ECT for my first major depressive episode, and when I took this class in the spring of 2008, it was just before my second major depressive episode that fall. My last treatment would be June 18, 2014, for my fifth major depressive episode.

The main side effect after the procedure, other than headache and nausea, is memory loss.

In college, and afterward, I forgot who I was.

But the doctors and nurses assured me that my memory would come back.

Lightning is an electrical discharge that takes place either cloud to cloud or cloud to ground. Most cloud-to-ground lightning is negatively charged.

I guess this makes sense. Negative stroke. Negative girl. Two negatives make a positive. I live another day.

Just like they said, my memory did come back, but it was tattered. And then it lay dormant until a volcano of flashbacks and dreams of abuse erupted. Suddenly, I knew more about myself than I ever did.

Yes, what a coincidence, there is a type of lightning that hovers around active volcanoes. Sacrifices. *Boys for Pele. Girls for Zeus.*

I couldn't let go of this ever-branching metaphor. Frankenstein's monster being reanimated by static electricity sparking off into a corpse, a human body. The human brain's neuronal lightning transferring memories, thoughts, actions.

After all, what meteorological phenomena don't happen inside our bodies already?

Now, I see lightning as the skeletons of girls. Girls dancing. Girls praying. Girls who've worn themselves and been worn down to the bones. Curved spines, long legs, spare torsos, bent knees, caves for chests, arms branching out into the world. Sometimes vertical, sometimes horizontal, sometimes between clouds like whispering secrets. Girls disappearing. Stick figures in their place. Girls running.

Predatorgirls with seven arms. Girls lost in a mirror. Each bolt is a shadow of myself in light. Bare bones. Guess the flesh. Imagine the bodies of each one. Create characters.

These are my body's blueprints, everygirl's.

Sticks of Fire

I grew up in the Tampa Bay area, the lightning capital of North America. I was raised on thunderstorms, watching the way the summer skies burdened and bruised themselves in the afternoons, the white hot fury x-raying the clouds, the visceral chill of hurricane-force winds, waterspouts conjuring off the coast like dancing smokewomen, and the facade of sunshine afterwards. These temper tantrums left small disasters in their rumbly wakes. These images and sensations collided together to form a hallucinogenic slideshow of an ordinary summer afternoon. Yes, roads and trees were askew, but mostly the aftermath consisted of a cooler evening with a sunset masterpiece eclipsing all ruin.

So go the meteorological mood swings of western central Florida.

Florida, the bipolar state. Where the northern part is the South and the southern part is the North. Confused. Oppositeland.

I've lived twenty-nine years in this state.

Tampa is a peninsula off of a peninsula. So is Pinellas County, where I grew up. Now I live in Tampa, surrounded by water yet connected to the mainland. Landbridges. Almost an island—only a flood away.

The heat builds up and sweat evaporates. Water rains down with a deadly light show and percussion. Taps from droplets. Timpani thunder. The music of storms.

> Circles and circles and circles again.
> Got a cloud sleeping on my tongue.[1]

"Tampa" is Calusa for "sticks of fire."

Those sticks are drumming on the air I breathe. Got a rhythm to my heartbeat. A clog in my lungs. The heat is a million leeches. I stay inside.

This screwy weather resembles my own weather. My mother's DNA gave me a cumulonimbus brain full of synaptic chaos and currents, an export from a German ancestor, and my father tried to teach me to read the minds of clouds.

Electrical currents are the blueprints for my thoughts, memories.

I wonder if my mind—my body's sky—lights up with its own lightning and if it vibrates with the thunder of recollection. Or do some memories stay silent too long?

Mississippis

I was eight and beginning third grade and I still rode my bicycle with training wheels. I've always been a late bloomer. After the summer of "the talk," I began to rid myself of the stigma of being the only baby in Mr. Sweetman's class who still rode with training wheels. It's as if I didn't trust two supports; four was better. Steadier. Safer. I didn't walk until I was eighteen months old—I crawled around, propelling myself with my knees and superior arm strength. My parents worried that I wouldn't walk before Tim, my brother, arrived. But I did.

The kids at my school had plenty of fodder already for bullying me: my short stature hinted that I'd been microscopic at birth, teachers announced my perfect scores in front of the class, my unsure teeth formed a jumbled smile, and my brown eyes begged for friends.

On the day I lost my training wheels, Dad taught me how to calculate the distance of lightning from where I was. I knew not to mess around in storms, but they occurred so often that it was difficult to muster up the appropriate amount of fear. The chances of being struck by lightning are about one in a million, but those odds are highest in the state of Florida. Ever the native, like my dad, I regarded storms as celestial landscapes, afternoon fireworks, a perk of living in Florida. My dad was cautious, nonetheless, and enforced basic safety.

Professor Martin Uman, author of a textbook on lightning, best summed it up: "Don't stand under tall trees, don't stand up in a boat, and don't go out on the beach during a thunderstorm. In general, don't make a lightning rod out of yourself."

As the dark clouds congested, Dad unscrewed the training wheels off of my bike and I teetered on two wheels. I wobbled to the end of Palmer Road and was turning back when I heard the sky crackle.

Droplets descended, and we stood in the garage, watching in awe as the thunderstorm stretched past the horizon.

"Want to know a trick?" Dad asked.

"Okay."

"Here's how you can tell how far you are from lightning: From the time you see the strike, count one mississippi, two mississippi, three mississippi, and so on until you hear thunder. For every mississippi, there's a mile."

The lightning was twelve years away.

Overdose

At fourteen, I was diagnosed with depression and obsessive-compulsive disorder. Still, I graduated high school with a 3.7 GPA. I spent a year at home attending a community college, then transferred to Florida State. After dropping all but one of my classes during the spring semester of my second year of college, I came home with my first major depressive episode.

May has the highest rate of suicides. On a Sunday in early May, I overdosed on 20 pink 0.5mg tablets of Clonazepam (Klonopin). Twenty: one for each pathetic year of my life. I smacked back the fistfuls after I'd counted them out. It had to be an even number. Water washed them down. Besides, it was 2006, and 2+0+0+6=8, my favorite number. I wanted to die.

Only I woke up. I'd collapsed in the den downstairs. My mother found me, yelled at me until I was semi-conscious, and insisted I tell her what I'd done.

"I overdosed," I slurred.

My mother didn't take me seriously.

"Get up."

I got up.

"…"

My mother commanded me to do something. I hobbled past the under-the-stairs closet and slammed my mouth into the wall. It took out half my left front tooth and a chip off the right one.

Each heave of a breath was a thought/task.

Spit out teeth.

Mouth fills with blood.

Taste red iron.

Swallow warmth.

Drink yourself.

Collapse.

Sleep.

Mother's voice on the telephone. "She can sleep it off. No stomach pumping necessary?"

Sleep it off.

I had to have a root canal the following Tuesday. It wasn't bad; I still had a bit of Clonazepam left in me to ward off some of the pain. I had a crown put on my left front tooth and a filling put in my right. I didn't look like Lloyd Christmas from *Dumb and Dumber* anymore. I looked normal again.

I slept for three more days.

An Introduction to Electroconvulsive Therapy

My shrink, Dr. W., was a wealthy, distant septuagenarian. I sat in the chair across from him; he sat behind his mighty, decorated desk. University of Florida paraphernalia and degrees abounded. When I had applied to transfer to a bigger school the year before, UF had rejected me. So I applied to Florida State and got in, just to spite the bastards. Now I was listening to this bag o' wrinkles ask me if "boy troubles" were to blame. In my mind I called him "the elderly sack of skin." Even though he'd known I'd been severely depressed for months and I'd nearly dropped out of school, it took my suicide attempt to convince him I needed electroconvulsive therapy. It was the famous "last resort."

I'd read *One Flew Over the Cuckoo's Nest*. I'd seen Jack Nicholson as McMurphy flop and quake on screen. *The Bell Jar* was my bible. I thought of Plath's horrific, poetic description in "The Hanging Man":

> By the roots of my hair some god got hold of me.
> I sizzled in his blue volts like a desert prophet.

As a kid and as an adult, I'd stuck my finger in a light socket and felt no spark. I wasn't the least bit afraid, just like I'm not the least bit afraid of lightning.

It couldn't be worse than the depression.

Floating in a black pool and drowning from the gravity of your own body, black mucus-water flooding your lungs, sinking the ship of your body, nothing to buoy you but the hope of letting go.

I let go once the general anesthesia kicked in.

Two of my family members have undergone electroconvulsive therapy: my great-aunt Juanita, my grandpa's sister, who complained of being "blue" all the time, and my second cousin George, who suffered from schizophrenia. Neither benefited from ECT. In fact, though it was reported throughout the family grapevine that George had slipped and fallen to his death, my mother and I believe he hanged himself and the family was trying to cover it up.

Both Juanita and George laid bare a common threat found in Pinellas County, Florida, the "Sunshine Skyway solution," I call it. Linking St. Petersburg, the southern tip of Pinellas County, with Manatee County to the south, the Bob Graham Sunshine Skyway Bridge is a four-mile concrete and steel pathway across Tampa Bay.

Its peak height is 431 feet, and as noted on its Wikipedia page: "Because of its height above the emerald-green Gulf waters, length of continuous travel, location in a warm-weather state, and modern architectural design, it is a popular spot for filming automobile commercials." It's even more popular for suicide. Juanita and George contemplated jumping off. The Baker-Acted teens I was hospitalized with at fourteen threatened to do it as well.

The last time I rode over the bridge, when I was twenty-eight, my boyfriend was driving, and I noticed red telephone booths every ten feet or so along the edge. This must be why they don't film car commercials here anymore—or if they do, they edit the phone booths out. I fantasized about plummeting into the bay waters, a very Floridian way to die, like dying in a hurricane, getting eaten by an alligator, or being struck by lightning.

ECT: A Brief History

I read up on ECT's backstory. In the 1930s, the age of psychoanalysis, biological psychiatrists competed for cures: insulin shock therapy, Metrazol therapy, and electroshock therapy. Italian psychiatrist Dr. Ugo Cerletti thought the hippocampus played a role in epilepsy and was determined to produce seizures in dogs to examine their brain tissue afterwards for any changes. Cerletti, aware that electricity could be used as a convulsive agent, placed one electrode in the dog's mouth and the other in its rectum and electrocuted it. The current passed through the dog's heart, so the animal died most of the time. Another psychiatrist, Lucio Bini, told Cerletti to put the electrodes on either side of the dog's head to avoid shocking its heart. Bini's assistant recommended Bini and Cerletti visit Rome's municipal slaughterhouse where pigs were knocked unconscious with electricity to make slitting their throats easier. They noted if the pig was not killed soon after the shock, it had a grand mal seizure.

And electroconvulsive therapy was born.[2]

The Procedure

The doctor shocked me, electrodes on either side of my head.
    Bilateral for a bipolar girl.³
I sing Tori Amos' song, "Mother":

> Green limousine for the redhead
> DANCING dancing girl
> and when I dance for him
> somebody leave the light on
> just in, just in case I like the dancing
> I can remember where I come from.

I have a grand mal seizure.
Because I am a dog.
Because I am a pig.
I think of another song by Tori Amos, "Blood Roses":

> Sometimes you're nothing but meat.

He doesn't slit my throat because, after all, I am human.
I blink myself back to life in the recovery room, not knowing how I got there. The blonde nurse slides my Mary Janes back on my feet and hands me my glasses.
My head is Hiroshima, post A-bomb.
Electroshock is no big deal.
It's only lightning.
I am the ECT capital of 28-year-olds.
I'm a goddamn marvel of modern science. Quoting McMurphy, the patron saint of psych patients.
You're so goddamn young, Patti Smith and Regina Spektor whisper into my ear.
But I feel so goddamn old.

I retreat into the waiting room. Some natural instinct and a nurse guide me on two feet. I drink the lukewarm coffee and eat the yogurt my father brought me from the cafeteria. We watch the radar on the TV, predicting the typical afternoon thunderstorms with green, yellow, and red blobs blanketing the state, foreshadowing the sticks of fire and the skeletons of girls.

1 Tori Amos, *Under the Pink*, "Cloud on My Tongue."

2 David Healy and Edward Shorter, *Shock Therapy*.

3 Doctors have debated my diagnosis. Today, it's bipolar II and obsessive-compulsive disorder.

EVERY HEAVY THING

JASON OCKERT

FICTION

I'm lying on your old bath towel upon the beach getting a tan and thinking about you—an open book in my lap—when a lizard drops from the sky and lands on my bare chest. This is where we used to go, back when we were we; a quiet cove away from both tourists and locals alike. You wondered why nobody came here but I didn't. I wondered why you bothered to wonder why rather than just enjoying what we'd happily stumbled upon: golden sand, ripe sun, frolicking waves, and inconsequential everything else but us.

We know why now, don't we? The story. The legend a passing fisherman explained to us one morning. You only half-heard him because he creeped you out with his alligator teeth and astronaut eyes. I listened. You once said I was a good listener. I remember. In the story, an *unwell* woman attempted to drown herself in the shallows just offshore. Lugged her backpack filled with every heavy thing she could scrounge from her apartment—a toaster, paperweights, iron, silverware, five porcelain birds painted various shades of indigo—and trudged into the surf. Apparently she used to dance. You might say she had a gift. She was engaged to a man who cheated on her—an oh-so-familiar tune, right? He did the infidelity mambo. When he called off the engagement she decided to call off her life. But she didn't drown. Kept her arms embraced in the straps for as long as possible, willing herself to hold on until the end. Couldn't, though. The body doesn't always obey the brain. Eventually she let go. Rose to the surface. Floated a while. Caught her breath. Then she dove back down to the backpack to fetch one other heavy thing. Swam ashore. Blew her brains out. Right here on our private sandy stretch of beach. Fisherman said—and you scoffed at this— that every few days or so the figure of a woman appears in the sand. A sandwoman. Said he'd seen it with his own eyes. The details are too clear for it to have been molded with a human hand, he claimed. Sand is stained red in a bloom around her head. Got her arms folded over her chest like how they arrange arms in a coffin. Or like she's still trying to clutch that backpack. Or maybe, and this is what the fisherman said he believed, she's trying to dig a hole into her chest and grab her sandy heart so she can rise up, fling it into the sea, and move on.

I can't tell if the lizard is dead. Might be. It doesn't weigh much. Though it rises and falls when I breathe, I'd have to stop breathing to determine if it could go it alone. The eyes are pinched-shut slits. He could be stunned or faking. I don't know. I don't even know where it came from. Nothing above but ribbons of cloud. It's one of those commonplace anoles capable of changing color from brown to green. Just an everyday creature I'd ordinarily overlook.

Do you remember the lizard story I told you? Back before we'd moved into our apartment? You were sad because you'd flattened one with your bicycle. You'd been biking along the sidewalk when the critter scuttled out in front of you and froze. When you swerved, it swerved, too. You said you could feel the tremor, all the way up in your handlebars, from its fragile bones popping. That seemed unlikely to me. What you felt was guilt. I know that now. Then, though, I did the *There-there-theres*. Talked reason. Explained how tetrapods have miniscule brains. They don't think like us. Like me. Then, as an example, I told you about my first experience with a lizard.

My parents moved us down to Florida—the kickstand of the country—when I was seven. There are no lizards where I was born. Back then I was intimidated by the way that the red flap on a male lizard's throat puffs out when he sees you. It's just his way of trying to seem more dangerous than he is, but I didn't realize that as a kid. On a balmy afternoon I decided I was going to catch one. I'd seen a teenager by the pool snag a gecko by wiggling the fingers in his left hand as a distraction and then thrusting his right hand out to capture it. Like the way you kill a fly. I tried the technique with a chameleon I spotted peeking from some palm fronds. My first swipe at it was tentative. Though I told myself I wasn't afraid, that was a lie. My hands were ready but my brain had reservations. What if it bit me? Were these things venomous? As it turns out, it didn't matter. When I half-heartedly tried to snatch the thing he dropped into the cranky grass and dashed straight into an air conditioning unit. The machine wasn't running. I remember standing there, a few paces away, hoping there was a safe place inside. There wasn't. In Florida, there's no rest for an air conditioner. Within seconds it came angrily alive. Then, before I had a chance to flinch, the lizard flew out of the unit, smacked me right in the chest, and fell to my feet. I stood there, stunned, trying to process what just happened. As I squinted down, it took my eyes a few heartbeats to realize that the little guy wasn't arranged quite right. His bullet-shaped head was angled at like ninety degrees. Still, he wasn't all-the-way decapitated. I ran inside, found some Scotch tape, and hustled back. Back then I didn't know the difference between repairable and irreparable.

In hindsight, I realize that I shouldn't have told you that story. It's just that you were so upset about the bone-popping bicycle incident. When I first started telling you I thought I might be able to make it sound funny. I mean, it's pretty pathetic, right? Me to the rescue with my transparent tape! You know how characters in cartoons try to stick their finger into a hole in a dam to keep it from busting but the fissures keep multiplying and soon the hapless fool runs out of digits and the dam explodes and everything washes away downstream? That's how I wanted you to see me. Somehow, though, I got off course. My laughter was shrill and ill-timed. When you asked, *What happened next?* I should have lied and said that, when I arrived on the scene—my hero's cape flapping in the wind—the lizard was gone. It wasn't hurt, after all. The light was playing a trick. The gashed throat was just his red flap warning me away. You deserved a lie. I wish I never mentioned the industry of those swift fire ants.

This book I'm not reading is *Zen and the Art of Motorcycle Maintenance.* You recommended it but I don't remember why. I've never even been on a motorcycle. The pages keep turning in the ocean breeze and I let them. This way I can pretend that I'm making progress. What I have read—several times now—is the brief note you left me. You wrote it on hotel stationary; a place where I've never stayed. Folded over, it makes a fine bookmark.

A funny thing I picked up from the fry cook yesterday—I may have mentioned Frank—is that if you stare at something long enough you'll eventually see a human face. He was talking about potatoes but he meant anything. Like, look hard at the underside of your arm and watch it morph into a face-of-sorts. He explained that this is coded in our brains. I was going to mention this after my shift but I got distracted, obviously. And hey, I wanted to tell you—and this is admittedly kind of weird—when I first saw the piece of paper on the kitchen counter I thought maybe it was a suicide note! Isn't that crazy? For a split second, when I read your note—*It's not working out. I'm leaving. Sorry.*—I thought you meant leaving this world! Like that girl with the backpack? Though, of course, you're nothing like her. Her note was undoubtedly better. She might have written, *My porcelain heart is a purple sparrow. I'm cracked and clipped and can fly no more.* Or, maybe she was bitter and simply wrote, *Fuck you, philanderer!* Perhaps she didn't leave a message and just let the blood stain in the sand speak for itself.

The anole on my chest is kind of grinning. Lizards are probably not as narcissistic as us and don't see reptilian faces everywhere they stare.

I wonder what he'll think if he opens his eyes. Will he be frightened, grateful, or indifferent? I guess it depends on where he came from. There are no nearby trees. No passing gulls have spit him out.

One time—and I already told you part of this story so bear with me—I was at a birthday party for this kid named Bubby. The mother had one of those helium tanks, the kind that pitches your voice into a squeak when you inhale and when you talk you sound like Mickey Mouse. Bubby and his friend Marco kept filling up balloons—there were like a million—until the birthday boy had a bright idea. He wondered how many balloons it would take to hoist a lizard into the sky. I was eavesdropping on a lawn chair in the corner while they speculated. The cake, as I recall, was awful and this fact struck me as really unfair. That was the first time I'd had bad cake. Anyway, so, Marco was the best lizard hunter on our block and he caught one cowering beneath the grill cover and, laughing, the boys looped the string around its neck and tied it super-tight. Though I know that lizards are not like us—you can't hang them the way you can a man—I still didn't like to see such bald cruelty. I stood up and said as much. That's when you told me to quit telling you the story because it was making you upset. You had a hunch that it wouldn't end well. I don't even know how we got on the subject in the first place. Anyway, I did as you asked and bit my tongue. I didn't explain that it takes three balloons all tied together to support an average-sized anole and that when those boys let it go—despite my protests—it lifted into the sky, soared over the rooftops and began rising. I clutched a handful of decorative stones and chased after it. My aim then, as it is now, was poor. The balloons were orange, red, and green in color. The lizard was brown. It floated into the blue, blue sky.

I know if you were here you'd have a theory. How it got here. You might suggest that he was tucked into the landing gear on an airplane departing from Ft. Lauderdale. That's what you would think if you were here because that's where you would've wanted to be. On an airplane, not in the landing gear. Leaving me to be with that timeshare guy. The stowaway recklessly scuttled out, couldn't hold on, and plummeted to earth. I am the X that marks the spot.

Since I'm getting everything off my chest here I should confess that you're not the only one with a secret. Something happened recently that I never mentioned because you wouldn't have believed me, and honestly I was too tired to try and explain. Late one night about a month ago, when you were away and I couldn't sleep, I decided to jog here, to our beach. I sat and listened to the hush of the waves. A sliver of moon dipped low and the sky was crowded with constellations. There were so many faces in the stars. Then, on my periphery, I saw something move. At first I thought it was a sea turtle or crab tunneling up for a midnight voyage. The disturbance was only a few yards away from where I sat. Then, as I watched, I saw a nest of red-tipped fingers wiggling around. Soon hands surfaced, then bleached-white arms appeared followed by a stringy mop of seaweed hair. When the head breached the hole and I saw her face, my heart nearly stopped. Her gaunt cheekbones were thatched with thin strips of skin, her grainy teeth jutted from rubbery, blackened lips, and unblinking emerald-colored eyes gathered all the light in the night and hurled it at me. I can still feel the weight of her gaze.

She awkwardly clambered to her feet and stood there with her shoulders hunched, head down, and bony arms dangling at her sides. A chunk of her jaw was missing and, when she turned away from me, I saw the gaping maw of her ventilated skull. The wind made a reedy whistle when it blew through her tattered dress. I stood up and prepared to bolt. But I didn't run, see? Although every instinct told me to flee, I waited. I gave her a chance to do whatever it is she needed to do. Which was, as it turned out, sway back and forth with the ebb and flow of the tide in a slow dance with the waves. It was dreamy and unreal. Peaceful somehow, I can't explain. I kind of rocked back and forth from foot to foot, with her, in a way. For a moment the beach belonged to us. Then she trudged into the shallows and became shadows, mist, and moonlight. I shuffled home to the empty bed. But now I'm back. I put your towel right where I remember her surfacing. She could reach up at any second, clutch me in her arms, and drag me into oblivion.

Hey, but guess what, Amanda? The lizard is still alive! Unlike all those others, he survived. He just opened his prehistoric eyes. Now he's bobbing his chin, nodding an affirmation. Telling me that he's all right. When he slides off my chest his sharp nails scratch tiny red lines into my skin. It doesn't hurt or anything. It's nothing permanent. Hell, if you look closely you can see that they're already fading.

WHEN TO STAY

RACQUEL HENRY

ESSAY

She remembers her father slicing into oranges in the backyard on days when the sun was high and blazing. How he taught her to sprinkle a little salt on top because that's what he did as a boy growing up in Trinidad. She remembers her mother taking her to Holden Park on sticky summer days and reading *The Secret Garden*. How she and her sister submerged themselves in forest and words. She remembers watching the Orlando Magic on TV and how she named the turtle they found on the side of the road after Penny Hardaway and Shaquille O'Neal. She remembers the heartbreak that is that team. She remembers sitting on the porch, Fort Gatlin across the way, and the pool and the children and thinking about how much she hates water, hates the beach. But she loved that Florida sun and the way it pressed itself against her skin.

She remembers how long it took them to get to Disney World because her family couldn't afford it when they moved from New York circa 1995. The relatives who would ask her if she visited the mouse and the beach often. She remembers how her lips would curl into a frown, how her eyebrows would wrinkle when she thought too hard about those questions. They were adults, she was a child, didn't they know that she had school and was just beginning a TBR pile that would never end?

She remembers the ugly parts, too. Like when Leslie Peters called her a nigger in the sixth grade and only got suspended for two days. A tap on the wrist. Or when she met the requirements for advanced classes, but the principal told her mother that she'd have to prove that she was capable anyway. And then the following year, she not only proved herself but had recommendations, and yet there were no advanced classes on her new schedule. She remembers that she still hadn't been good enough.

She remembers the lines of agony in her father's forehead whenever he came home from being pulled over *again*. Her father had always been her father, but it was then that they made her see the line in the sand. Then they made her notice that his midnight skin, shades darker than her own, would always sound the alarms. She remembers how her mother would hold him so tight like she was afraid that tomorrow she might not see him walk through the door. She remembers the time her sister got thrown out of a bar because they were over their *black limit*.

She remembers wanting to be away from that hometown. She moved away for ten years to try to forget it. Every year she burned another memory. She kept putting more people, more trees, more bodies of water, more dirt, more time, whatever she could find, between her and the city. But those old memories rose like ghosts, kept calling for her, stretching their arms out for her to come home. And so she did.

She knows that there are other cities. But when she sees her roots in places like the old Marble Slab on Colonial, or the high school with the Brave head on Kaley Street, and the Panera on Michigan and Orange where her sister went to skip school, and the Fashion Square Mall where she and her best friend would drink Jones sodas on Saturdays, she knows that she's home. This city is hers.

SKETCH NUMBER THREE IN INK

JOHN BRANDON

FICTION

Boyd might have chosen the office park because the flat-faced, featureless buildings looked impossible to scale, a worthy challenge. Or because the complex was out of the way, unguarded, in fact nearly forgotten. Or because each one of the eight buildings was identical to the others in height and aspect, each with an almost perfect lack of outward purchase, each with an absence of transcendent architectural ambition—non-special, they were, both generally and in comparison with their brethren. He'd conquered, Boyd, in every corner of our hill-less state, quaintly painted water towers and soaring bridges and grim cathedrals and white-bricked university libraries, and by that point, getting oneself up into the under-reach of the sky with no tools one wasn't born into the world with—well, that was already growing passé. See, this all took place during the lividest throes of irony (*Irony?*), mere months before the bubble burst, when nothing but nothing was allowed to stand in its own natural, plain light, when nothing could unblushingly betoken only itself, its function or beauty or hallowed mystery, when all was ripe for parody, when all was low fruit for the grubby fingers of satirists, vulnerable to insincere glorification and snide undermining. Maybe irony isn't the word, or isn't precise enough a word—there's always a better one if you take the time to sift for it—but what we know is that the objects and notions of life seemed, then, shuddery, scuffed, sheepish of soul—corner diners, dismemberment rock, hearses, stucco half-slums, even Northeastern brusqueness, nautical garb, the frosty misgivings of chaste young women, family reunions, cheerful den-fires, tremulous rage, winking as romantic overture, wooden rocking chairs, the perfect panic of chased young women, Italian-suit-wearing drug lords, cornpone, croquet, prudential motives, the madness of artists, hoity-toity card games, regional neckwear, buzzcuts, silk pajamas, clumsy first dates, ennui, the blue light of dawn, Texas, innocent hayseed effrontery, adolescent high-achievement, princesses, libertinism, the Lord our God's promises and even His premises, martinis, the buoyant but defeated philosophies of prostitutes, clay roads to nowhere, circuses, geopolitical brinkmanship, robust beards and military mustachios, Fellini and (naturally) Godard, kind wishes for strangers of the road, foreshadowing and denouement, flop-haired and doe-eyed surfers, delicious villainous smirks, the events of the play *The Crucible*, Zen.

Our town is somewhere near Orlando, so there's that. I won't tell you the town's name, but I'll provide you its coordinates. 28.5x81.2. Temperature: sweltering. Snakes: venomous and fed-up-acting. All our male residents have last names for first names, and this has been the practice for generations immemorial, well before it became the fancy in Kansas City and Minneapolis and Houston and Little Rock and Spokane. My name, for example, is Bettencourt. My father's name is Renquist. My grandfather's is Summerall. The boy—a boy still, most would agree, at the time of his summiting one of the slick, sulking edifices of Grove Royal Business Plaza; a man *now*, though only a handful of years have passed, living in Las Cruces and superintending a fleet of refrigerated trucks—this person, this male human, whose form constitutes the focus of Sketch 3, is named, as you know, Boyd. The names of females in town aren't really notable, except there was a girl my year in school named Cinderella and one named Bruna.

Cinderella became a maritime lawyer and Bruna a very talented waitress. Not that the town is on the water because it isn't, or known for elegant restaurants because it isn't. We're known for our uncles, more than anything. Like in a lot of settings similar to this one, uncles are countless. They overrun the place. You know their type, these men. They lack social grace in a way that's to their credit. They're not so good with money, but this fact doesn't anguish them. Once the sun is gone, they smoke. They tell jokes that are right on the border—positively teetering on the razor's edge of decency. All our uncles are bestowed a nickname by their niece(s) and/or nephew(s). This is a sign of respect and affection, the devising and use of the nickname. For instances: Uncle Gravy, Uncle Tightknot, Uncle Squirrel-Dog, Uncle Red-Titty, Uncle Colonel, Uncle Fever. Uncle Rorschach. Uncle Pearl. Uncle Seymour Hoffman and Uncle Holmes and Uncle Neckbrace and Uncle Five-a-side and Uncle Mercado Negro and Uncle Sport-fox and Uncle Aficion and Uncle Ken-tuck. And what else? Hmm. What other true thing can I report that modern urban readers might find enchanting? Well, we natives have this verbal peculiarity where we say 'myself' after the participle—I think participle might be the right term but maybe it's not—in cases where most people wouldn't. Such as, if you asked why we didn't answer the phone, we might say, "I was outside exercising myself" or "I was back there masturbating myself again" or "I make a point of showering myself every time it rains." Sometimes our language is old-fashioned, like how we call our household possessions—books and herb pots and shoehorns—we call that stuff our 'moveables.' At times we talk like airboat guides, and at other times we shake the thesaurus with such vigor we hardly know, ourselves, what we're trying to mean. We have a cultural blend of such extremity it's hard to even know how to speak about it. Some of us are tattooed with Cole Porter lyrics; some of us work in tiny pull-through banks about the size of food trucks; some of us have haircuts like roosters. My step-grandmother is half-blood Calusa and couldn't get sunburned if she sat naked on a tin rooftop the whole month of

July. The flowers in spring and summer are blue-violet, spoiled butter-colored, tongue-colored, regular candy pink, and all conceivable shades of off-white. The clouds, when they blow over, are tight bruised fists. The night sky is purely starred and close and somehow makes one squint as much as the midmorning glare. The roads, all but the main highway that ducks through, are winding.

The Figures

Boyd—About Boyd, I'll not say much. He's very tan and has silken yellow hair that, were the sketch finished in oils, would show up heavenly and golden, a halo with a cowlick. His sneakers were always crappy, but that isn't of much moment because when he climbed he went barefoot. Lean of build, like you could handle him in arm-wrestling but he could triple you in chin-ups. Earned a C in every class he ever took at the high school, eight semesters worth of flawless averageness—maybe an exaggeration, an aspect of a mythology—but the point is nonetheless valid: the dude didn't fancy being fancier than his fellows. His father, Turner, drove a mosquito-control truck for the county, those parade-speed yellow behemoths trailing clouds of white noxious gas over parking lot and playfield and beauty parlor alike. Whenever something didn't go Boyd's way (but not something consequential, I'm talking something like his football team was flagged for holding on a twelve-yard out-route or he bought rotten pecans or he got out on the pond and then the thunder started up) he would say *Sweet Whore of Padua*! It amused him, after one of the universe's frequent small reversals. Myself, I say *Oh, bother*, but I say it in the voice of a pompous Londoner. Or I say *Get in the car, Ethel!* Anyway, Boyd wound up marrying one of those terribly beautiful women it's best not to try and describe, so I won't, too much—the type that when you first glimpse her feet and ankles and calves, you just know, with only that to go on, that she might be the most alluring creature you've ever beheld, and then with due trepidation you guide your eyes up, a nudge higher, a nudge higher, and bothered whore of Padua if you're not right: effortlessly dazzling in every perceivable detail. Lithe but capable fingers, gleaming teeth, rumba hips. Posture, but posture wouldn't even matter. (I've seen maybe two-dozen of these women in my lifetime, but I used to work charters down in Palm Beach County.) The one that chose Boyd was from a couple of coasts, neither of them nearby: Virginia, by way of Spain. She saw him writhing up the cliff-face of a monolithic glass condo building in Miami and that was enough for her. Hook, line, sinker. She was landed (in ownership of part of the earth's surface), and after she saw Boyd, she was landed (deprived of ownership of her heart). I don't think it ever occurred to Boyd that *he* had a choice in the matter. When a woman of that order selects you, you just go. You march where that graceful, entitled, manicured finger points you. So, to put it neatly, he went from storming the side of one of those reflective blue towers to being caged inside it. Top floor. A puma in a drawing room. Not happy of soul, but also aware that he was not, bodily, in a gripe-worthy situation. Nobody would've wanted to hear it. All the rib eyes and oysters he could cram down his gullet, sleeping between sheets equal in value to his car (his former car) with a woman whose hindquarters would writer's-block the Bowles family. He eventually got his bearings and asserted himself to the tune of moving them to Las Cruces, which was to them, as it would be to most everyone, starkly neutral territory. He pawned a hands-less platinum bamboo-banded wristwatch she'd bought him, losing thousands of dollars in the exchange, and informed her he had one timepiece and only one and would never wear another, which was a reference to a staid, old-style, straight-dick Rolex his deceased Uncle Carlos Valderrama had presented him at age twelve or thereabout. In the sub-basement of New Mexico, I'm to understand, the wife's beauty is regarded gravely, something she doesn't own but stewards for the benefit of others like an emissary of pleased gods; while for Boyd's part, the combination of his past as a famed independent alpinist of glass and steel and stone and treated wood, along with his mastery of so many chilled boxes full of plenitude and health that shuttle about the poor, cracking pan of the desert, along with his corralling in his bedchamber a rare manifestation of ideal feminine form...well, they consider him something apart, a man to stand still and observe as he passes on the street, and I suppose they're right.

He told me, after we'd both moved away from town, when I ran across him in Arizona, that he'd climbed things because the exhausted after-dreams were choruses of refracted golden light. His words.

Browner—Browner is of the generation preceding mine, a contemporary of my father's. He's the other figure in the sketch, the one whose feet are booted and planted heavily on the dust-kissed marl of Central Florida, rather than the one whose feet are bare and cling (left) and dangle (right) fifty feet above. Browner was famed for his lack of bitterness. Deservedly. My father used to tell me stories of the man's prep baseball prowess—tales perhaps, many of them (like the straight C's of Boyd's), but some of it can't be exaggerated. You can't exaggerate an official batting average: .417 as a junior and .461 as a senior, that latter mark the all-time standard for the district. You can exaggerate the bite on a breaking ball, but 21 strikeouts in a game are 21 strikeouts in a game. A state championship is a state championship, the only one our school ever won in any consequential sport. He dislocated his shoulder stealing third in the state semifinal his last year (and actually finished that game and played in the next, the final—obviously, or we wouldn't have prevailed) and after the season was vanned over to Tampa to have the shoulder operated on. Well, the surgery went smoothly but the recovery decidedly didn't, and the rest is history that never had a chance to happen. One infection after another, like they were standing in line at the jerk truck licking their chops, and by the time it was over Browner's shoulder socket had shriveled up like an old lady's. He couldn't toss a grapefruit across a kitchen—those are my father's words. But then came the amazing part: he just carried right on. No staring out a window at a sun-brittled barn. No more ardent spirits than was usual. No self-help seminars. No sobbing on the phone to ex-girlfriends. No binging on Hostess Cakes. No dramatic purging of sports equipment from his home. He was eighteen years old and wise enough to understand that a prolonged vigil for his old life wouldn't get him a new one. He was offered a job as a sheriff's deputy and took it on the spot, did the training over at the county seat (yes, Orlando) right along with the other greenhorns like he'd never for a second hoped for more, wore the uniform with chest-puffed pride, the mirrored sunglasses, the pistol buttoned in its black holster, sat in the cruiser at the speed-trap for hours at a stretch, rented an apartment, grilled burgers, hung clocks and posters, even watched baseball on TV, if you can believe that. It was the most unexpected victory he'd ever been involved in, this non-acknowledgement of tragedy, and he'd been a part of some doozies. He could smile as readily as anyone, but not *too* readily; it wasn't like he'd lost his marbles, like a man whose only son commits suicide or something—he was just content, fielding the tasks of his life one at a time, laying off the balls and swinging at the strikes. By the time I knew him, he was older. He was nicer than your average cop, everyone always said so—willing to listen to all sides of a story, willing to distinguish between malevolent intent and foul luck—and this was with all that lost potential in his background. The millions of dollars. The travel. The swanky hotels. The women. The sunshiny hours of physical competition. The plush retirement that, by the moment memorialized in the ink-sketch, he would've been blithely ensconced in. Some months after being deputized, he married a woman a bit older than he was, ten years older to be precise, retired now (*now* now) herself and doing fine, who then owned a little one-truck carpet-cleaning business. Strong arms and dark straight hair. Nice lady. She hadn't known of Browner when he'd been a star of the diamond—why would she; he'd been in high school and she was grown. Browner told my father once that she didn't like to touch him at all except when they made merry, which experience she required each morning upon awakening and each evening before she slept. I'm sure there's symbolism to be strained for—maybe not symbolism but some sort of felt-slippered narrative furbelow—in the fact that Boyd ascended barefoot and empty-handed the facades of great buildings, while Browner's wife strode back and forth inside them, dragging each floor with her equipment, the two of them toiling on connected but perpendicular planes (though likely never at the same point in time, and likely not the same buildings), one cleansing the fibers of carpets and the other stretching the silk of his soul…well, that's milk I'm electing, at this juncture, if none object, to leave inside the cow.

To Browner, as he explained to my father the next day, the episode with Boyd had been a matter of religious freedom, but that meant the climb, the feat, had to be performed in the mode of unsullied and sacred devotion. He'd yelled up to Boyd—though if he'd only wanted Boyd to hear him he needn't have raised his voice all that much—that he would be permitted to finish his upward pilgrimage unmolested by any agents of law so long as the crowd immediately and permanently dispersed. You see, a clutch of huffers who'd been poking around for a secluded party spot had happened upon Boyd and had alerted some of their associates to the spectacle, and by the time Browner showed up there were dozens of black-jacketed community college dropouts milling about the curbs and outgrown flowerbeds beneath Boyd, who'd by then reached the sixth floor and had two yet to vanquish. Browner said everybody had to clear off, and that he would too; he'd be the last to leave. He said Boyd, once he reached the roof, had one Federal minute to do whatever he needed to do up there. Sixty ticks. He was leaving that to Boyd's honor. Boyd had that five-pound wristwatch; Browner could see it all the way from the ground, glinting even in the dusk.

I was talking all this over with my father just the other night, on the phone, and finally I said, "So what's the moral?" It's a joke we have. I don't remember when it started. Just something we say when a conversation reaches its last steam. One of us says, "So what's the moral?" and the other always answers, "Don't eat yellow snow, unless of course you're allergic to regular." (Part of the appeal, I think, is that we're both rank amateurs when it comes to snow.) So I was surprised when my father clammed up a moment and then took a ponderous breath and told me, "Nothing that happens to you can derail your life. Whatever happens to you *is* your life." After another pause, in which I could hear the hollow tocking of some wooden wind chimes I'd hung on my balcony, he added, "If you think nothing's happening, you're the biggest fool of all."

And also this: My other step-grandmother, not the Calusa but the other one, is very Catholic, and as a child I'd get dropped off for weekends with her and she'd take me along to mass, my hair wet-combed into a part and squeaky laceless shoes on my feet, and even at eleven years old, or whatever I was, I understood the whole grand potboiler, the coil entire, when I saw those soft-padded kneeling-rails that flip down from the pew in front of you. The customer must be kept comfortable, even when prostrating his unworthy soul before the Almighty. That was the moral *that* day, and I didn't need to ask anyone.

I have eleven more of these sketches, if anyone wants them. (A coworker of mine calls them mud-potted anthems of rectitude, and, smart as I am when I put my shoulder into it, all I can do is red up and chuckle at that.) They're each laden with very accessible lessons, but also they affect (right, *affect*?), when absorbed as a complete series, a greater edification in the open-hearted that's tricky to put into words and perhaps shouldn't be, by me or my father or anybody—gumption concerning proper manly positioning in this changing world. Decency and grit. These are the forums at issue.

Orlando, now, is simply a town hustling up a living like any other, relieved to have been audited and judged and moved on from, to have been jangled upside-down and italicized and at long last left be, pleased enough to just tickle the tourists, fill the sinkholes, trim the greens, widen the roads, grant licenses, and live to see another day.

Pleased enough to have its laundry out on the line and everybody took a good gawk and got back to their own damned rackets.

Me, I'm living in Delaware. For a job. Those anonymous business campuses, like immortalized herewith—they boast about eight thousand of them in this state. And they do have some gals up here you wouldn't mind watching load the groceries, if you can get yourself over near the ocean.

And finally, at the risk of being obvious, there are of course ingredients of the universe that irony could never, under any circumstances, ensnare with its slick hungry appendages. Like, purely for example, the humbling vastness of night in the lowlands. Or the seedy scrape of a wooden boat against a wooden dock.

ALL RIGHT, NOW, CUPID

SOHRAB HOMI FRACIS

FICTION

My self-summary

Taking a turn onto Stockton last month, I saw a pedestrian stumble off the curb, almost into the path of my Sonata, and stagger back onto the sidewalk. He was a blind man with a long folding cane, and on his own. His shirt was tucked, unusual in our increasingly hipster neighborhood. Alarmed by his misstep, he was sweeping the path frantically with his cane as he lurched ahead through his personal minefield. It broke my heart.

I was on my way to Bold Bean, but I felt my coffee could wait. Looking for a spot to pull over, I noticed a woman walking the other way. She appeared to be out for a stroll through Riverside, just taking the air on a sunny day in a below-the-knees skirt. Slowing up at the light, I turned to see her go straight up to the blind man and put a hand to his arm.

He jumped back at first. I've tried to imagine what life would be like if I were blind, even gone about my chores with an eye-patch on. But it's impossible to know. Can't say if blind faith would come easier to him or harder. I have friends who are atheist—I'm agnostic myself, happy to believe in the incredible yet credible universe.

I felt that the universe had brought her to him. As the light turned, I saw her take his cane hand in hers, stilling his jumpy moves and speaking to him quietly. I caught the look on his face as he listened. It was a beautiful thing.

What I'm doing with my life

I know, that wasn't exactly a self-summary. But if it had been, what would be left for these other spaces?

So: what I'm doing with my life.

I don't even know what I'm doing on OkCupid. I'm retired. From a downtown-Jacksonville bank, a year ago, and glad of it. You wouldn't believe the politics at our branch. A teller caught in the middle was fired and went postal. You might remember it from the news. If not, I've got the inside story: see *The Six Things I Could Never Do Without*. It's my Charles Bukowski story. Did you know his postman character, Chinaski, was really him? That's my kind of fiction. What's the point if it's all just made up? Chinaski's something of an ass, but still. Consider this an advance entry for *Favorite Books*.

I'm really good at

...not doing things when I'm expected to.

It's part of why I never married. I understood why women wanted that, but I knew a couple who were great friends for a while, then did well enough in a relationship, then split within a year of getting married, then hated each other through the divorce, then became friends again once the exponentially increasing expectations they'd heaped on each other finally fell off their shoulders with a thud.

At this stage of our lives, though, I imagine women have less need of marriage. The window for raising a family has shut. It's just about us now.

The first things people usually notice about me

They don't usually. Notice me. When Ralph Ellison wrote, "I am invisible, understand, simply because people refuse to see me," he might as easily have been speaking of a retiree as a black man back in the '40s.

You know what I'm talking about. My accurately stated age didn't stop you—even though retired is as good as dead, online—nor did my weathered face, my balding head, or my talk of old-fashioned folk in tucked shirts and longer skirts. You must know what it is to have aged in a young people's world, maybe even a youthful neighborhood.

I've heard it hits women earlier, not long after the bloom is off the rose. Comes as a shock that they've no longer got it and men aren't all over them anymore. The male gaze suddenly ignores them.

But now, online, middle-aged women find they still have it: backlit by the screen, glowing, in demand again, approached not just by a handful but a hundred lonely men. So it's hard for men to be noticed in the crowd of thumbnail pics and messages left unread. On the other hand when *you* message us, it's an occasion. We notice.

If you've got your bloom back, you probably have no need of me, and I hope the right guy's in the pile. But then why would you be searching profiles; why are you reading mine? No, if you're here, you're either past that second blossoming or you don't care for the crowd.

Favorite books, movies, shows, music, and food

Well, neither *Invisible Man* nor *Birdman*.

The hero I want is Retiredman. And/or Retiredwoman. Cue a softer, melodic theme, not *Birdman's* driving drumbeat. Michael Keaton is still too engaged, too vigorous, too straight-backed, too quick-witted, too ambitious, too accomplished, too attractive to attractive women. He can still fly.

So maybe *About Schmidt*, then. Its gently rolling but not-dead-yet score could be mine, if anyone thought my life was worthy of a movie. The trouble with iconic actors like Jack Nicholson is that I usually can't see past the famous face. But Schmidt was real for me, from the establishing shot of him at his office desk waiting silently for the end of his last sedentary workday to him throwing out his back on a waterbed to him crying over the letter from young Ndugu in

Tanzania. I don't know if you have children. I don't, but I've come to see my continuity in all boys and girls.

Food? Prime Rib. Spanish Omelet. Swiss Cheese. Chocolate Decadence... I remember them fondly.

The six things I could never do without

...but have to. See above. Add hair. Also resilience and a few remaining principles. Without the one, I couldn't survive; without the other, I wouldn't want to.

I know, loan officers aren't thought of as principled anymore. Funny thing: we used to be the villains for declining loan requests; now we're reviled for having accepted them. I know a lot of loans were handed out in the name of the American Dream, then foreclosed on when the subprime bubble burst. I'm ashamed for my profession, but that wasn't me: as far as I know, the people I put in homes still live in them; the ones I put in cars still drive them. That I never made management is a reverse badge of honor.

Remember those branch politics and the fired teller? Tellers are walking dinosaurs who already know the asteroid is about to hit. Dating is not the only thing that has moved online. In the 2010s alone, mobile depositing has climbed a thousand percent. And that's on top of ATMs taking over half of all deposits and counting. Tellers are now at a forty percent share that's dropping like a stone. This particular teller was an old hand who'd seen the slide begin. He'd seen his hourly rate inch up over decades in which the cost of living soared. He saw neighboring credit unions pay their tellers one-and-a-half times that rate. He had reason to be vocal.

Management knew he did, but that didn't mean they liked it. They told him he had a bad attitude. What does that even mean, he asked. Don't bite the hand that feeds you, they said. Nobody feeds me, he yelled; I'm not a dog! And they fired him.

Until then I'd walked a line between the factions, but this disturbed me. I'd seen the man come in day after day for years, exchanged nods and small talk with him. Now his words, in the tone of a man at the limit of his endurance, rang in my head. I dropped in on the assistant branch manager, a generally levelheaded person. But she shrugged and pointed mutely at the branch manager's office. A good decade younger than me, he said he respected my opinion but he'd been left no choice.

The teller may have felt the same. What happened next was unheard of, so no one saw it coming. Bank robberies still happen, though even that lovely tradition has gone online. Or, disturbingly, the victim of a predatory loan kills himself and/or his banker. But a teller? Our branch manager probably thought he was back to beg for his job. Instead he shot the branch manager with a handgun. Thrice. First in the chest, then twice up close, in the head. Then he shoved the barrel in his own mouth and splattered his brain across the office. The sound, indoors, was like fireworks. I won't disturb you with the other sounds. By the time a security officer rushed in, their blood had pooled together.

The next day I sat at my desk in a daze, then turned in my notice of early retirement. I could do without the job. It was killing us. The assistant branch manager, looking harried out of her mind, talked me into staying on for three months. And then, finally, I shed my suit.

I spend a lot of time thinking about

...the past, sorry. And yes, that includes the women in my life.

Funnily enough, not the women I was in relationships with (though I think of them, too) but the ones with whom I couldn't be. They hadn't lost all potential to work out, in my head, just most of it. That's 'ones,' plural. If it was just the one, you'd be worried. You'd move on to the next profile. Still here? I'm starting to like you. That potential to work out, for us, is still intact.

On a typical Friday night I am

Friday night, Monday night, it's all the same when you're retired. I was never a partier, anyway, especially once the bank stayed open on Saturdays.

That doesn't mean I don't get out. I don't want you to think I have no friends. When one stays single this long, a lot of one's friends wind up being empty nesters or couples who never had kids. It's good to get male and female company in a package deal with no strings. It's bad when a woman who's weary of being with one man 24-7 makes it so apparent she prefers my company that it makes him edgy. Sometimes she's younger than him and still has the bloom. He enjoys that, but it makes him insecure and tired of the competition she attracts.

I, for one, know my boundaries, so they've seen that and settled down. Old dogs are less territorial. On the rare occasions I've brought a date, the men showered her with attention, and that was all right. Turnabout is fair play. So you might have that to look forward to.

The most private thing I'm willing to admit

Right. It's so private, I'll just put it online. Sure, it's anonymous, but not once we talk.

Here's a bad thing to admit on a dating site called OkCupid: I don't know about love anymore. It depends on so much. Timing, attraction, reciprocity, fidelity, durability, and so on. Two-way street all the way.

When the light on Stockton turned green, I wanted to stick around to see how it went between the blind man and the older woman. It looked like good timing and a great start, but who knew? Either of them might have had somebody waiting at home. As to attraction, it looked like they were feeling each other. Literally. But it might have been no more than the basic good-Samaritan interaction.

About attraction: its nature morphs as we age, doesn't it? In *Birdman*, Michael Keaton's screen daughter, Emma Stone, still in the first act of life, is horny for Ed Norton. At her age, all I cared about was how pretty and/or sexy a girl was. Norton, arguably on the verge of the second act, middle-age, is having relationship problems with Naomi Watts. By then, it wasn't only physical anymore. That part of it never went away, but sometimes I wished it would, that I wasn't so indiscriminately drawn to the bloom. Now I wanted a woman who was also kind, on the same wavelength, great company, and so on. Warning bells, not wedding bells, went off in my head at the slightest discord. Keaton, nearing the other end of that second act, is divorced, and even his fling with his stage costar, a younger woman, is failing. By that point, I'd come to terms with our inherent imperfection, my own first of all.

So here I am, at the start of the third act. And everyone knows, in general, how that ends. It's only the particulars that vary. My friends put it bluntly: "You're gonna die alone." I tell them I know. And I'm not the worst company. They've given up trying to set me up in the real world, bless them, but they sat me down to toss my hat into this virtual ring.

I'm looking for

See above. Microscopically detailed checklists are a problem, and they're ubiquitous online. Everyone's looking for everything, in some precisely imagined composite character. Height, weight, age, marital status, eye color, hair color, race, religion, location, education, occupation, income, nature, interests, sexual prowess—he or she must have it all. But s/he who insists on a 100% Match usually ends up in a sing-along with Bono: "I Still Haven't Found What I'm Looking For."

Take my first OkCupid date: we were a 95% Match. She was a well-kept brunette, bloom almost intact. Never married, no kids, sort of like me, but in her 50s, still in the workforce. Business writer for an insurance company. So we went to see *The Big Short* in the remodeled old Five Points theater. They've annexed a neighboring store and turned it into a second auditorium—have you been in it? Coziest little date theater, maybe five rows and fifty seats. We're sitting there in the semi-dark watching Steve Carell and company, sipping our wine, when I notice what she's doing with the large bowl of drizzled popcorn in her lap.

She keeps her face hovering over it, peering hard to sift and pick and toss aside or move to her mouth one popped kernel at a time, working rapidly but steadily, kernel after kernel, missing scene after scene. Occasionally she transfers a piece from the bowl to the running table in front of our seats, where it joins other discards. In the flashes of light from the screen, I can see them and they look fine to me. I've been in and out of the bowl for intermittent snatches, and all of it tastes good. My heart sinks.

Still, once she lays the bowl on the table, she's laughing at the financial machinations of Ryan Gosling and Christian Bale, so maybe the date isn't going badly. Except I'm not laughing. Just about then there's a vignette about Wall Street newbies trying to get in on the credit default swaps action. They're snidely put in their place by a hotshot insider. My date laughs again, so I crack a wry smile and say, "Schmuck." It takes a while before I realize that she has shifted away and stopped laughing, that she was laughing *with* the poser, not at him. I think. At any rate, I didn't survive the sifting process. So much for the 95% Match. What the fuck, Cupid.

You should message me if

...you haven't run for the hills.

After the light turned green on Stockton, I dawdled with my eye on the sidewalk. No one behind me yet, though cars could turn off anytime from Riverside Avenue. The immediate question was this: now that the woman had stabilized the blind man, would the two carry on in opposite directions or would they proceed together?

Even as a small stream of cars took the turn, I got my answer. She swiveled around, linking her arm with the blind man's free arm. I cheered aloud and set my Sonata rolling. Once across Oak, I swung into the lot of a convenience store reassuringly named Best Choice. Taking one of only a handful of parking spaces, chancing a tow if I wasn't back soon, I eased out and followed the pair on foot, a quarter of a block behind.

I reasoned there was a good chance the blind man had come from St. Catherine Labouré Manor, a sprawling assisted-living place back there by the river. In which case, she wasn't just taking him back to his home. And linking arms felt more intimate than if she'd taken hold of his arm. I saw that he'd folded his cane away, so now to someone who didn't know, they looked like any elderly couple out for a walk on a gorgeous Florida day.

Outside of the car, warm currents sifting through hedges and trees brought me their green scents. I tried shutting my eyes for a moment, and the fragrance grew, as did the sound and feel of my shoes on pavement. The man and woman were chatting; I caught their companionable tone as we passed the Zencog bicycle store. Then they turned onto Myra, so I hurried past coffee drinkers outside Bold Bean, my original destination. My back and I were enjoying the unexpected exercise, and I was more interested in *their* destination.

Rounding the corner, I could see them again, closer now. I'd been down Myra before, even financed a home or two on it. It was a charming residential street with a random mix of houses. Wooden, brick, stucco, stone, burgundy, lime, blue, salmon, freshly painted, weather-stained, ranch, two-story, gables, terraces, porches, car porches, tidy, ramshackle, manicured, overgrown. But it worked. I could see either the man or woman at home here, and I was no longer sure which one it was.

Approaching Osceola, they slowed. Not to cross, but to turn onto a driveway. I quickened my pace. Behind palmettos and flowerbeds stood a modest single-story home in adobe with white trim. Its windows were trellised, its roof terra-cotta. I wished the man could see it. But the lawn smelled good, and as I passed, I saw he was smiling. The woman was helping him over a pebble path, so that had to feel good. At the door, she let go of him to get her keys out. He stood quietly by.

IN PRAISE OF THE GREYHOUND

NATHAN DEUEL

ESSAY

'd been sleeping rough for weeks, through the sparse wilds of central Florida, where I had to contend with black bear, boar, tornadoes, and an army of biting insects. Then I reached the Gulf, and the powder-soft sand of the so-called Redneck Riviera. Through Panama City and a series of Air Force bases and military installations, I walked past condos and barber shops and bar after bar, through traffic night and day.

Then, in a building thunderstorm I limped across a massive span over the Intracoastal, from a barrier island and into Pensacola, and on the edge of this city I balanced on a log, near an un-built lot surrounded by McMansions. I fell backwards onto a pile of rocks. Whipped by a sudden wind and hounded by bugs and pounding rain, I scrambled to my feet and pawed through my foul-smelling bag. A tent pole had snapped. So I looked for something I could use in its place. My hair dripped into my eyes and my hands were ripped up from thorns, but I found a pretty good tree branch and spread out my tent and used this branch to hold it up. Inside, sweating, with the rainfly inches from my face, I lay back and dreamed of the Greyhound bus.

I'd have kept walking forever. But I needed to go home. And so walking back home would have taken too long. My situation was due to an agreement I'd made with my wife years prior—in which the two of us would never be apart for more than four weeks.

We tried going longer once: Nearly six weeks, when Kelly went to Singapore for a reporting assignment. The first seven days, I felt disoriented. The second week: sad. That third stretch of seven days I started going crazy, ranting and raving, bouncing between feeling manic and hopelessly depressed. But by the fourth week, something happened. I found I'd gotten good at being alone. By weeks five and six, when Kelly and I talked on the phone, it was like talking to someone new. At the airport, I wrapped my arms around a stranger.

This was not ideal. So I sat in a collapsed tent, on the edge of Pensacola, ready to go back home. It had been nearly four weeks since I'd last been back. In the morning I'd wake up, walk seven miles or so, and I'd push open doors to a bus terminal, and because I wanted to find out who I actually was more than I wanted to change into someone completely new, I'd exchange money for a seat on one of America's unsung glories: The Greyhound, a creaking web of 3,800 stops along a long-haul network that connects every remote corner of this country, from Eutaw in Alabama to Wolf Creek, Montana.

Picture a ten-hour or twenty-hour or even five-day trip, if you're aiming, for instance, to get from Miami to Skagway, Alaska. If you are rich or in a rush or rarely if ever called to our nation's dustier corners, you probably haven't ever had to bother with Greyhound. It's also possible that fear or deep poverty have delayed your first ride. In any case, a ride on a Greyhound can be more than transportive.

An airport is increasingly a militarized zone on the edge of any metropolis—hard to get to and fortified by vast armies of security and at the same time not really that safe at all. It's not a real part of our lives. Strange, exceptional things happen at airports. Giant metal tubes hurtle through the air at 600 miles an hour. The other day, a guy wearing a Zorro mask managed to alarm security personnel at a Los

Angeles airport to such a degree that within an hour the whole airport was shuttered and no flights were landing or taking off.

This would never happen at a rural Greyhound terminal. These are places that work, with departure times that will not be slowed by some guy with a mask. You can get a decent sandwich, probably, and a tank of gasoline and a spare tire and maybe a pound of fresh crabs, if you're near the water. More than likely, the guy who climbs aboard in a Zorro mask mainly wants to visit his Aunt Mildred in Biloxi.

It's the variety of people you might sit next to and the fact you share a cramped space for so long that is so key to an experience I happen to love. Greyhounds get you from here to there, but the central feature that makes them so slow—and so worth thinking about—is how often they stop, and where, and how each time they creak to a halt you and everyone else on board are forced to think about the very idea of progress.

We can't all walk across the country. Even a guy walking across the country, such as myself, needed to take a bus now and then. I walked that direction, thinking. Everything I'd been doing by quitting my job months earlier, walking all day, every day, and now heading back to New York was about not being in too much of a rush. In my old life, I'd always wanted to go faster and there were so many ways to gain more speed. Out here on this walk, things were slower and the way to measure success was inscrutable, if it existed at all. Never was it part of the plan to walk away entirely from my wife Kelly.

Weeks could go by out here and what I found was a kind of meaning in a moment. It might be the respect of four vehicles taking their time at a stop sign in North Carolina, or the sound of a bird taking off from a pond in South Carolina, or the sight of a dog licking another dog's face in rural Georgia. If you tried quickly to consider what actual value of any of these instances might have, it probably seemed like I'd lost sight of something. I wasn't sure that was right.

I could have just flown back. But there was a delicious insanity to taking the bus that seemed to match the core stupidity of walking in the first place. In a funny way that helped me not get too cocky, the act of taking a bus helped suggest I hadn't really gotten anywhere yet.

On a bus, to be sure, I'd be moving more slowly than on any plane. The rides take so long there's time to think, to grow, to become a different person or at least hold onto and think about the version you hope might be emerging. You can ask and answer questions, of yourself and others. A variety of ways to live is right next to you and one of them probably wants a cigarette and maybe some of your pie, if you happen to have any pie. Greyhounds tend to feature riders carrying good snacks. And babies. If there's a screaming baby beside you, you might be handed that baby. As opposed to a plane—all lightning and magic, balls of flame and cold steel—a bus operates on a human scale, and our relationship to its physical speed makes it feel more connected to the way we actually live, day by day, screaming babies and all.

The whole experience speaks to a different era. There's the lo-fi pageantry of the employees, especially the conductor, who wears a special cap and maybe a v-neck sweater, too, all of it made more regal by the slickly tailored-blue coat with the red piping and the shiny name badge in the shape of a sleek racing hound. (This outfit changes now and then, but at its core is the message: Old-fashioned care.)

There's style and ceremony, too, in the boarding process itself: a human ritual of taking a paper ticket and making sure everyone is seated and firing up an old engine and extinguishing the incandescent lights and then going through the announcements, chief among them that no liquor is allowed on board.

Because things can go wrong. There's almost always someone getting drunk. The buses are rarely in the best of shape. If one breaks down, as it did for me one time on the way to New York, they'll eventually drive over a new one. If that one breaks down too, you might wait a while, but somehow you'll get there. One driver on a doomed bus years ealier, for instance, calmly announced the engine was on fire. He signaled, pulled over, and while the bus glided to a stop and burned, we took the opportunity to have an impromptu picnic on a roadside in what I recall as being rural Mississippi but could also have been Utah.

Georgia, Mississippi, a crossroads in the remote desert of Utah. I treasured all the times in my life I had the good luck to go slow. At a time when airports shut down from the slightest provocation, when cars drive themselves, and there is more than one app to summon a person who will pick you up without even expecting you to talk to them, I am proud of the moments in my life when I've had time to move around the country by Greyhound.

This time, I maybe needed the bus more than ever. I had walked all the way across Pensacola and pushed open the doors and felt like I had no more to give. I had no job and little money but this was a place where I could rest easy. Anyone could take a bus. At a terminal in Pensacola, the low rumble of air-conditioning muffled the sound of snoring and coughing, from people patiently waiting for whatever came next. Above us, a flickering set of fluorescent lights cast the chairs bolted to the ground in a white glow. A security guard eyed me. For a moment, I wondered if I'd sunk too low. Was there too much blood on my socks? Torn leaves in my hair? Did I smell too badly?

"You left your water bottle at the fountain," he said, pointing helpfully.

I was so excited to see my wife, to reconnect with New York City, to rest up and get ready to come back. I still had 700 miles to go.

Because part of the agreement I'd made with Kelly long ago was about coming home. The other equally grave burden was to go back out. She always did—to Singapore or Indonesia, Iraq or Yemen. Now it was my turn.

I looked out the window as the world went by, put at ease by the steady way we were moving. Every other car on the highway went faster. Everything about the bus said take your time. Every three hours, there was a stop: Jacksonville, Savannah, Charleston, Charlotte,

Richmond. I began to feel like a version of myself I could be happy with. I was man who had left, who could go back, and would almost certainly return again.

In Richmond, we all got off the bus, filed inside, and lined up at Bay Number Four. The driver disappeared—which wasn't the end of the world. With such long drives, you encountered shift changes; no one driver could handle all thirty hours. But then a mechanic boarded our bus—with all our bags still on it—and he drove off. I could feel my chest tightening. A few minutes later another bus took our slot. Passengers bound for Harrisburg pushed us aside.

I thought about New York and everything I'd left behind. I thought about the meager posessions in my bag, and the unpleasant sensation of caring too much about where this bag currently was. I pictured the bus and my bag and I started to get impatient and then I felt a growing tide of upset.

"Fuck it," someone said, and he stalked outside to smoke. Maybe the bus would never come back? There was something exhilarating about not knowing.

So much of life is about winning and control and knowing. Somewhere in my anxiety about leaving New York, somewhere on a multi-day bus trip, I might figure out there was a compromise between hoping this walk could go on forever and the way it would eventually oblige me to come up with whatever came next.

With a crew of people I'd met in Pensacola, I laughed and listened to crickets and smoked cigarettes, and the humidity burned off and the heat of another sun came up.

UNDOING

ALISSA NUTTING

FICTION

arnie had to get the bloody sweater off her father. He was crying, watching a twenty-year-old camcorder video of himself with Marnie's mother—footage of the two of them riding a giant mule at a county fair. He kept rewinding the video back to the scene where they jumped off of the mule in tandem. He'd pause it there, so it looked like they were being sucked upright into the air, the two of them levitating beside the mule. Then he'd press play, then rewind, then pause. Her father found this activity gratifying. So much so that he'd recently quit his job to do it full-time.

Her mother had run off with a jazz musician several months ago, during the first week of Marnie's junior year of high school. She hadn't left contact information or been in touch since.

Marnie considered trying promiscuity as a distraction from grief, but was hesitant. It felt like her mother leaving increased Marnie's chances of an unwanted high school pregnancy. "Think about it," Marnie told her friend. "Say four girls hook-up with four football team members under the bleachers Friday night. All four guys pull out slightly late, but only one of the four girls gets knocked up. It would be the girl whose mother had abandoned her." Marnie had the sense

143

that stigma did not readily consent to solitude. The disgrace of her mother leaving was a lodestar. A GPS that sent Marnie's coordinates to further misfortune.

She figured traumatic desertion probably increased one's fertility. There was a magnified picture of cellular division in her biology textbook, and below it the book's previous owner had written GREED in red marker with teardrops coming off the word, like the letters were sweating. Maybe whoever drew this hadn't meant it as a caption for the photo, but Marnie felt that was the best interpretation. She could imagine the dumb, animal brain of her body thinking it had figured out a way to solve the void in her family. One person left me? No problem; I'll make another!

It was best to stay vigilant against supernatural interventions like pregnancy, which seemed as eerily magical as her mother's overnight departure. Wasn't magic just the act of appearing or disappearing, suddenly? The sadness that arrived when her mother departed played tricks on Marnie. When her father had told her, he'd said, "Children shouldn't glimpse such uninhabitable honesty"; in his despair his bathrobe had fallen a little too open. Although she didn't think of herself as a child, the statement seemed apt in regard to many aspects of her life. Panic now came upon her at school in sweaty fits, and when the urge to vocalize grew too intense to suppress, she'd burst out in laughter to camouflage the hysteria. Marnie kept two halves of a broken pencil in her backpack to hold out as prop evidence as she cackled and shook. I'm always breaking pencils and cannot help but laugh at the frequency! Fractured wood, how hilarious!

Pretending to laugh produced the same abdominal soreness as repetitive vomiting and made her smile muscles hurt. Between classes she liked to go into a bathroom stall and stretch the flesh of her cheeks out like pizza dough. As she kneaded her face, she'd remember a song from childhood whose lyrics pretended English words all became Italian words with the suffix of –uh. It had been funny when she was little, but its lyrics lacked cultural intelligence. And it was mean, its main character 'uh big-uh fat-uh lady-uh.' She saw now that the song was awful.

Perhaps this was the work of growing up, Marnie thought: increasing the ability and speed with which she could recognize the bad. She thought often of Puffy, a hamster she'd owned for two years in elementary school. The day they'd brought it home, her mother had washed it in baby shampoo so its fur had a floral smell. Marnie played with Puffy for hours, and then he defecated on her lap, which was a shock. Marnie hadn't realized the hamster was going to defecate. Ever. She'd wept for hours, became withdrawn for weeks. Nothing was perfect.

Marnie's friend Jana felt her boyfriend was perfect, though. "He's so good," she was always telling Marnie. The boyfriend was older and had been fired from a fast food restaurant over allegations of theft from the cash register, though Jana staunchly maintained his innocence. Marnie had the feeling that over time, problematic information about him might come to light. Jana had recently gone on birth control, and she was very alarmed at how small the pills were. "Do you see?" she'd asked, holding one out to Marnie on the tip of her finger, "how microscopic these are? I don't think they're even big enough to work."

"Yeah," Marnie had agreed. "They should be way bigger."

Her mother's abandonment seemed to have given Marnie access inside a whole carnival tent of unwanted discoveries. For example, she learned that Gam-Gam, her paternal grandmother, had never been in favor of her parents' union. Gam-Gam had a lot of opinions. She visited the two of them a few weeks after Marnie's mother went away.

No matter what Gam-Gam was saying, something about the tone and volume of her voice made Marnie feel like she was being ordered to mop a floor. "Of course it ended in disaster," Gam-Gam yelled at Marnie's dad. "You married for love! Next time set yourself up for success," she encouraged, adding that he was welcome to borrow the recipe she'd used for her own marriage to his father, now forty-eight years strong: he needed to seek out a tepid emotional connection, a person whose skill sets and interests were in direct opposition to his own. "Because happiness isn't going to cut the mustard," Gam-Gam continued. "There is no way in hell."

In terms of gossip, Marnie found out, dying was preferable to leaving. The dead can be hard to speak ill of, but no one had that problem regarding her mother. "I heard your mom is a slut," a boy said at lunch. "Are you a slut too?" She couldn't tell if it was a bullying tease or a straightforward inquiry. When she didn't answer he began eating a meatball sub at a fast-forward pace. Marnie wasn't sure why, but she'd held out a napkin out to him. He didn't take it. Instead he wiped his forearm across his mouth and got sauce all over his skin. It looked like an injury. "What are you staring at?" the boy asked. Marnie didn't answer but continued to watch him. It was strange to see a person who appeared to be hurt eating instead of screaming or weeping. She wished her father would try eating. Due to the bloody sweater, her father now also seemed to have surface wounds on his body.

After he had stopped going to work, Marnie had waited up one night until she heard his snores. He liked to pass out on the ground in front of the TV, watching the tape, then wake up and resume. He often watched it while lying on the ground in corpse-posture, limbs sprawled out, seemingly the fallen victim of a swift homicide. He'd wake up with a red-patterned indention on whichever of his cheeks had pressed against the carpet all night. Every morning half his face appeared cloaked with a mysterious birthmark.

Marnie had taken the tape out of the player, gone outside and thrown the tape in the creek that ran out along the back acreage of their property. When she came back inside, her father was awake and the same tape was playing on the TV. "I have several copies," he said, "but where's the one you took?"

"This video thing," she'd offered. "You're trying to do something with time?"

"Do you see that?" he'd asked, pointing to the screen. "Your mother's eyes? Don't they seem to be looking into the future? Did she think our love was destined to fail even then?" Marnie had glanced at the paused image. Was her father talking about her mother, or about the mule? Both looked unimpressed and a little hungry. They were squinting even though there was no sun.

She'd turned off the TV and they'd stared at each other. "What are you wearing?" she'd finally asked him. It was a small white angora cardigan, buttoned but stretched beyond capacity; it ended several inches above his midriff. "One of the only pieces of clothing your mother left behind," he said. "I had to put it on. Does that seem crazy?"

There was a free calendar from the credit union, several years old, that her mother hadn't thrown away because it had a motivational quote on each month's page. Whenever a question puzzled her, she used to open it and read a quote aloud by way of a response. Marnie had looked at her father and flipped to June: Unhappiness is in the eye of the beholder, it read. "I wouldn't use the word crazy," she'd answered.

When she told him the tape was in the creek, he'd suggested they walk there and go fishing for a few hours. It was three a.m. on a school night. Marnie didn't like fishing; it seemed like fishing might be the only thing more miserable than standing in the living room with her father, which made her interested to try it. She liked challenging herself this way: On any given day, how much discomfort was she able to bear?

They took one reel with a lure and Marnie watched on, her father having promised to throw back anything he caught. But when the line did pull and he tugged up a bass, this vow proved hard to keep: it had swallowed the hook. The hook was caught on something deep inside the fish. She had to turn away while her father struggled to get it out. In the dark the blood looked like ink. The average-sized fish was leaking so much of it that in another context it would've seemed comical—her father's arms and her mother's sweater looked like they'd been drenched in gallons of fish blood. "Okay," he'd finally said. "It's good as new."

Marnie had disagreed. They'd watched the fish's body float out across the water like a tiny canoe. Then it gave a twitch and they both gasped: "There it goes," her father said. "It's going to swim away." But it was just a death lurch, or maybe something from below had poked it. "We're not going to find the video tape," Marnie said.

"Hey," her father added, his face perking up with suggestion. "Let's go inside and watch it?"

On the walk back to the house, she remembered a day, unremarkable, when her mother had worn the sweater. She knew her father wasn't going to take it off willingly. He'd continue to wear it, and when the blood dried he'd act like any problem Marnie had with the garment had been reconciled. She'd have to take it off of him one string at a time, unraveling a little bit of it each night.

"Can we let the video go to the end this time?" she'd asked him. Her father wasn't interested in the most terrible event captured on the tape, which played out in the shot's farthest right corner during the final moments of the recording.

The last three minutes of the tape went like this: he and her mother jumped off the mule. They approached the camera and began talking about their upcoming wedding. But in the very distant background, the mule made a slow but immediate beeline out toward the palm tree lawn and started to give birth. "Why were you riding a pregnant mule?" Marnie asked. "Not just one of you but two? That seems cruel." Maybe, she reasoned, if her parents hadn't given a pregnant mule trouble they'd still be together.

This made Marnie hope her parents hadn't made a video recording of her mother giving birth to her. It wasn't the thought of the delivery on tape that made her skin crawl as much as the idea of her father pressing rewind and then play, again and again, reversing nature's decision. It seemed like the type of obsessive careless action that, under certain conditions, could cause Marnie to cease to exist.

"Did your collective weight induce the mule's labor?" Marnie questioned. "Be honest with me!" Her father cleared his throat and pressed rewind. On the television screen, the mule's faraway body retracted the suggestion of life it had been pushing out. When the creature turned around, it seemed to have changed its mind.

DISPLACEMENT: A LETTER UNADDRESSED

MICHAEL J. SEIDLINGER

ESSAY

I leave a note, unsure if anyone will notice. Really, I wouldn't care if they did. But then five miles out, I find the note in my pocket, unfinished and unaddressed, and I wrestle with the urge to turn back. I tell myself that I don't care because it's true—I don't. Look at me: I don't care.

This far out, with only half a tank of gas and the sixty, maybe seventy dollars if I counted all the change I've tossed in the glove compartment, my chances are that I'll get about as far as the city limits. I'll pass the theme parks and the strip malls until all I see is the road. And the road continues for as long as I want.

This isn't really even my car. I mean, it was given to me, but I didn't pay for it. My name might be on the title, but someone else, who will remain nameless, pays for the insurance, paid it off, and has paid to keep it well-maintained. Does this mean I'm driving a stolen car?

Yeah, okay—I'm turning around. It's different, the feeling of returning rather than departure. Leaving feels almost hopeful, bittersweet if I let it sink in. The road returns me to the street corner where I stood around drinking from a bottle in a paper bag, with people I could have called friends if I stuck around long enough to remember their names; they went on about the show we had just been to, a show by some local band I can't remember but, strangely, still hear their songs echoing through my mind.

On either side, there are whole stories where I could easily play a small part—I know for certain that I've watched a few films at that Regal theater there; you bet I could be one of those people standing around at that Planet Smoothie across the street, wasting time before show time. Sushi Hanna, that sushi place where I'd go to sit at the bar, mostly because it was quieter than everywhere else, able to sit and have a drink and never get carded. Maybe because they remembered me, but more likely because they *really* needed the business.

No matter that I'm nineteen. No matter that a whole year has passed without much momentum. Something holds me down, keeps me here. Well, tonight is different. The strip malls are sprinkled amidst different suburban neighborhoods. Everything's green, planned out, cul de sac, roundabout, floral street names, the road itself, continuing to bend and buckle as it carves through the manmade wasteland. Really, I haven't been anywhere, but still, I have an inclination that wherever this road takes me, it'll all be the same.

Guess I'm feeling pretty hopeful, you know.

The billboards often act as waypoints, letting me know more than any street name or stoplight where I've been versus where I'm going. The billboards for Cracker Barrel and a local radio station and something by Ralph Lauren have been passed over, traded for billboards about the return of the McRib, a new Starbucks latte, and some mattress warehouse that probably remains in business because it doubles as a drug front.

I'm young and I have so much to say. I'm young and anxious and worried and nobody. I'm nobody and I really just want a one-on-one with the world.

This place sickens me so I speed up, pulling away from the thought. What's the lifespan of someone who knowingly has no free will? Think about it because I can't. I'm too busy avoiding this stupid fucking car going twenty-five in the left lane.

There's a reason why people living here remain indoors most days, where the central air keeps you comforted and there's no day or night. There you get the faintest sense that time is infinite. It feels like you can go at your own pace, and there will most definitely be a tomorrow, and clearly a day after that. It feels so comforting to think that the days aren't numbered. I feel my heart quicken at the thought, which makes me want to speed up, but I need to keep an eye on the tank. I'm burning fuel like I'm going to be fine.

I eye a nearby bar—it's closed because everything here closes at midnight. A few places stay open until two. It isn't a city for night owls. This is no place for those that put sleep on hold. I'm wide-awake, mind-racing, just looking for the next objective. *There's nowhere to go.* Truth? Of course not. Forget that I've been driving for hours. Ignore the fact that it really sounds like I'm going in circles.

I could always find a park and sit there in the dark for an hour. Wait until dawn approaches and the various breakfast places open up. I just can't keep driving around like this, not without a clear destination. I need some time to get my thoughts straight. I feel restless. My knuckles are white, palms raw and red. I pass a billboard advertising a nearby Denny's.

Speed up, speed up, I tell myself. I hold my breath, my body doing the opposite of what the mind tells it. The car slowing to a crawl, I end up staring at the high school's all-too-familiar outdoor hallways, how everything about the design of the place accentuated its upper-middle class culture; a private school for students with promise, from families that all have made the most of their careers. I used to go here. I can vaguely recall what it took to become someone else in order to fit in, a version of myself not unlike me, but different enough to keep people guessing, unable to really figure me out.

Was I happier? Do I miss those days?

That Denny's is the same one I used to go to twice a week to avoid people from school, mostly people from final period study hall. I'd sit in the back and sip coffee while everyone thought I was at band practice or something. They knew me for what I wanted to become.

A half tank of gas wasn't ever going to get me anywhere. Either I can keep pretending that I didn't think this through or face the fucking facts. Nothing to see here.

Totally not someone that has no idea what he's doing.

Not at all a person that's feeling really stupid right about now.

Don't look. I'm going to figure this out.

I pull up to the house, putting the coupe into park, doing my best not to make a sound. Not that it matters. Lightless inside, they're all asleep. They've been asleep since nine. How predictable. So much to see and do and yet it never changes—their routine outlined to occupy a small little sliver of the world. I guess I'm a little resentful.

I have to get my shit together. And how can I do that if I stay here, doing what—taking online classes, going to community college? That road goes in circles. It goes *nowhere*. It'll end with me living, at best, a few miles away in some apartment, with a roommate that I do my best to avoid, while I work some job I don't care about, one that pays the bills but doesn't give me any pride in what I do or promise in life.

I kill the engine. I pick up and read the letter, angling it away from me slightly to catch the nearby streetlight. It reads exactly like what it is—an angry letter written by a self-proclaimed runaway.

What am I running away from? I really should go back inside. No reason not to. There's a bed, a whole room full of memories I'd never admit to anyone as being full of nostalgia, the sort that could take hold, keeping me in the moment longer than I'd like. It's the sort of feeling that makes me feel like, sure—maybe I could get used to this.

The letter's embarrassing but it gets one thing right: I can't get used to this. There's no future here. I'm alone in this. I'm alone in my choice to leave.

I need to feel like there's something more, feel like I am actually getting somewhere. I have an idea of what that might be, and it's a collision course of rejection and anonymity that lengthens to stretch past the road. Depending on who you are, it might go on for longer than your lifetime. I'm talking about the struggle. Yeah, struggling artist. I wrote that in the letter. I'm a cliché. Part of the reason to leave.

I tear up the letter and let the pieces fall into my lap. I watch one particularly small piece get picked up by a gentle gust of wind, carried out the passenger side window. I watch it disappear and think about my own disappearance. Surely there hasn't been just the one. My life is a series of disappearances. And it's my hope that there'll be plenty more. One day, I'll wash up to the surface as someone you'd never expect.

DUMMY UP

KRISTEN ARNETT

FICTION

The elephant at the dinner table was a mannequin wearing crushed blue velvet. Her face was cherubic, cheeks ruddy with pearly pink paint, lips stained crimson against the jut of her white teeth. All the dark hair on her head was combed into a French braid, a plait so thick I couldn't help but compare my own thin hair and find it lacking. The three of us held hands while Mr. Kinson said the blessing, the mannequin's fingers dry and cool in my right and his warm and damp on my left. He fed her sips of wine and bits of linguine, noodles dandling off the fork and dragging against her slick chin to leave a stain shaped like a serpent's tongue.

"Please, call me Brian," he said, dabbing at her face with a cloth napkin. He folded it neatly and placed it back in her lap. "Cecilia insists."

I thought of my mother, alone in her darkened bedroom—lights out before eight, wearing the same ratty nightgown she'd had on for the past week and a half, hair greasy from not showering. My father's ghost played havoc with our memories until none of us could stand to use the bathroom where he'd hung himself.

"Brian," I said. "Could you please pass the garlic bread?"

155

•

In counseling, the first thing they teach you is you need to let yourself grieve. The problem with that rule is you're already grieving; it's a wound that silently weeps below an ill-structured bandage. You're walking through the grocery store, leaving droplets of blood when you see the cereal your father liked to eat late at night while he watched the late show. You soak the passenger seat of the car as your mother drives past the bowling alley where your father hosted your eleventh birthday party. Grief isn't a popped balloon; it's a perpetually dripping faucet.

Before my weekly group sessions, my mother would drive me to get pizza at a restaurant we'd never been to with my father. We'd sit at the red vinyl booth next to the front window. I'd choose the side under the golden O in Tony's Pizzeria; I liked the way the darkness would enclose me in a ring, cupping me like a shadowy hula-hoop. I'd usually choose a slice with pepperoni. My mother always picked a Greek salad and gave me her olives.

Sometimes we'd talk about classes or my brother David, but mostly I just watched the kids walk past on their way home from elementary school. There was a crossing guard across the street from where we sat, a woman with short, dark hair and very tan arms. She'd stand patiently while the kids gathered on one side of the road, then truck them across with speed that belied her age. Once when we were getting in our car to leave, I noticed her face was pitted with ancient smile lines.

"Take these." My mother scooped the olives with a round soup spoon and dumped them on my plate.

One rolled off onto the paper tablecloth and I squeezed it with my fingers until it bled salt. When I bit it in half, my teeth dug into the pit. I felt the tension deep in my gums. "Thanks."

"I don't know how you eat those. They look like eyeballs."

"You're gross." I bit into another and then took a bite of my pizza.

"Have you thought more about summer applications?" She didn't look at me while she asked this. She was staring at the man behind the counter. He looked a little like my dad, sallow skinned with half a beard grown in.

"I haven't decided." There were a few band camps that I'd attended last year, ones my father had picked out. He'd played saxophone in high school. Pictures showed a thin, happy guy with a lot of dark hair and big dimples. I played trumpet. Our only resemblance was in the shape of our eyes; both so narrow and close together that we sometimes looked cross-eyed.

"Let me know. David's already decided on lacrosse and basketball." She did look at me then. There was unevenness in her skin tone, patchy pinkness on her cheeks below her reading glasses. "I think it would be good for you. Get you out of the house."

"Okay. Maybe." I unscrewed the cheese shaker and carefully coated my slice in a thin layer of parmesan dust. The residual grease turned into an orange paste.

Most of her salad was uneaten when it was time to leave. She'd only picked out the feta and a few fragments of romaine. The rest she'd stuff into the fridge, where it would wilt over the next week, until I took it out with the rest of the trash.

My mother handed me the keys. "I'll meet you outside," she said, and walked into the rear of the pizza place, toward the restroom. I didn't need to follow her to know she'd throw up the little bit she'd choked down. In the past seven months, she'd lost almost thirty pounds.

Our car was parallel parked between a gray minivan and red sports car. It sat like a beige lump between them; a shapeless, decade-old Honda that would have been mine, but instead of my mother getting a new one and me getting the old one, we'd become a single car household. My father's Acura had gone back to the dealership.

The sun baked the pavement and my legs looked pasty and pale in my jean shorts. People always asked where I was from, like I'd moved to Florida from some dank place in Europe. Leaning back sideways over the center console, my legs hung out the open door while I waited. I could see the sky and some overhanging tree branches, oaks that dipped low and grabbed for each other across the small street.

There was no breeze. My face felt sticky and hot with humidity as the blood pooled in my head and pounded in my feet.

Legs hovered overhead. Long, perfectly tan legs with strappy white sandals and a matching skirt fluffing around them like the floppy petals of a flower. The legs floated there, disembodied, as I stared and blinked and stared some more. Then there was a torso and a neckline. I sat up, all the blood rushing back out of my head until my eyes went spotty and dark.

The gray door of the minivan stood open. A man placed a mannequin into the back, laying the stiff wooden body down flat on a blue and white plaid quilt. He adjusted the limbs and fluffed a pillow, smoothing a sheet over the torso. When he stood back up, I saw that the man was Mr. Kinson. His expression was calm, the same as he looked at our group meetings—brown eyes liquid and sympathetic, jaw relaxed under a beard a shade darker than the hair curling over his shirt collar. There was a large sweat stain under the arm he put up to slam the trunk, darkening the gray pinstripes of the fabric into black.

We made eye contact through the windshield glass of my mother's car, neither of us acknowledging the other. He reached into the front pocket of his shirt and pulled out some mirrored aviators. I looked over to check for my mother and, when I turned back around, Mr. Kinson had already climbed into his minivan and was driving away. I imagined the mannequin all bundled up in the back, buried under the quilts, bumping around the floorboards like someone's hostage.

We sat alone in her dressing room. Me and the mannequin. Julie and Cecilia in the glow of early evening, both us clutching highball glasses full of bourbon, though hers was strapped to her hand with a tan strip of velcro. Mr. Kinson was cooking dinner—*linguine with spicy marinara and muscles, Cecilia's favorite*. It was important for us to get to know each other a little better. *Cocktails*, he said. *Bourbon is a great social lubricant.*

It was less a dressing room and more a walk-in closet for vintage movie stars. The walls were covered in powder blue wallpaper embossed with gold and ivory print. It smelled like potpourri and expensive shampoo, the kind you get at a salon. Buttery halogen light bulbs surrounded a slick vanity with a built-in cheval glass mirror the size of a family tabletop. Cosmetics covered the surface, lots of lipsticks and powders, expensive perfumes in cut-glass bottles with cork-lined stoppers the color of weak tea.

Cecilia perched in a padded brocade chair in front of the vanity. I sat on a tufted ottoman in the center of the room. On every wall hung racks of clothes. Hangers dripped clothes, dresses in all kinds of fabrics, shelves of expensive shoes—high heels, silky ballet slippers, wedges. There were robes trimmed with ermine and marabou feathers, sequined bags, and slick ropey belts that looked like someone had skinned a snake for them. My fingers drifted over a cream satin slip edged in baby pink lace.

"Pretty," I said. "Really nice."

Sipping from the glass, I clenched my teeth against the burning in my throat. The bourbon tasted awful, but at least it was cold. "What are you going to wear for dinner?" I asked, taking another sip. There was light classical music playing from speakers set into the ceiling. "I guess I'll just wear this old thing."

I was in the same clothes I'd worn to sculpt. There was clay flaking up on my knuckles and chalked around my short fingernails. The jeans were already dirty; I'd worn them for three weeks in a row, not wanting to deal with the mounds of clothes piled in our laundry room. The t-shirt was one of my old ones from marching band two years ago—back when we'd done a routine to Blood, Sweat, and Tears.

"Would you mind if I borrowed something?" I asked, getting up and stretching my back. The alcohol coursed through my veins and made me feel fuzzy and sexy. The air was pleasant and warm in the room, a solid seventy-five degrees. I flipped through the rack against the wall opposite the mannequin and watched her from the corner of my eye. If I squinted enough, she almost felt like a real person.

We were expected to document everything in group, the before and the after. Photographs, of course, but also journal entries, random memorabilia, slips of paper where we'd jotted down phone numbers and email addresses, even a ratty stuffed bear snatched off someone's bed. There was a lock of bleached hair and a deflated birthday balloon. We archived and scrapbooked for reference. Though we were young, we'd all experienced heavy loss. It was a kind of drowning. None of us were nice to each other. None of us were friends.

"Whose turn is it to talk? Lindsay, take the walking stick."

There was an empty chair beside Mr. Kinson; he'd set his full mug of chamomile tea on the wooden seat and just left it there, the steam lifting in soft curlicues. I kept expecting him to excuse himself and bring out the mannequin, but he just sat there, only getting up once to bring over an unopened box of tissues. Nobody ever needed tissues.

It was an art therapy group, but I was never sure what "art" was supposed to mean. I played an instrument and there were a couple of girls who danced. One of the older guys was involved in local theater; they'd just put on a production of *As You Like It* at the high school. If anybody painted, they didn't do it at counseling.

"Go ahead," Mr. Kinson said. "We're all listening." He leaned back casually in his chair, one leg propped over his knee. He was wearing basketball sneakers that didn't look like he'd ever worn them outside. His socks were dark with little red triangles on them. They made his ankles look bony.

"I don't want to go today." Lindsay was my age but went to the private school across town that cost twenty grand a year. Her black hair was cropped close to the scalp on one side and she wore a lot of red lipstick, but it never stained her teeth. She leaned heavily on the walking stick, what we passed around the circle when it was someone's turn to talk. It was made from mahogany with a monkey's head carved into the top.

"We'd really like you to share what you've brought." Mr. Kinson gestured at Lindsay's seat. On it sat a feathered masquerade mask. When she picked it up, it dangled awkwardly, side-heavy and lopsided with sagging peacock feathers.

"It was Lauren's. My sister's. She got it when she went to Mardi Gras last year."

"And why is this important to you? What does it makes you think of when you look at it?"

"I don't know. It's pretty." When she lifted the mask, gold sequins glittered from around the eye holes. "And my parents were really mad about it; she said she was gonna go to our aunt's house for spring break. I guess it makes me think about how she always did whatever she wanted and didn't give a shit what anyone else thought."

"Anything else?" he asked, reaching out for his tea, then changing his mind and leaning back again.

Lindsay shrugged and sat back down.

A dedicated shrine to the deceased sat in the corner of the room. We'd each had to place a picture when we first came to group. The picture of my father was one of him mowing our massive backyard. He was in the army reserve and always wore a green camo shirt when he did yard work. In this shot, he'd been halfway across the yard with the sun at his back, haloing his body in a golden corona. My brother was halfway out of the shot, bending over to pick up clippings to stuff into a black garbage bag. On the crown of my father's head sat a giant leaf, like a baseball cap. I couldn't tell whether he was smiling.

"Anybody else bring something?" Mr. Kinson picked up his mug and held it between his palms. The steam had long since run off. When nobody responded, he stood up and finally took a sip. "Fine. Let's just go ahead and plan on Micah and…" He looked around the circle, making eye contact with me. I didn't look away. "Julie. You both bring something next week."

No one said anything. People slowly gathered their stuff and checked their phones. I waited until everyone had nearly left before

I got up and followed Mr. Kinson into the kitchenette at the back of the hall. It was bright back there, the overhead fluorescents flickering like a strobe light. Mr. Kinson dumped the rest of his tea in the sink and began to scrub out his mug with one of the tough green-backed sponges that were ancient and graying.

I thought of the mannequin sleeping in the back of the van, in the Florida heat, her body heating until her painted skin bubbled. Maybe her makeup would smudge the pillow, the kind of drunken mornings I'd seen my mother have recently—empty bottles of wine and beer lining the bottom of the recycling bin until there wasn't room for our microwave dinner boxes.

There were still two inches of coffee in the pot next to the mini fridge. I picked up one of the little white Styrofoam cups and filled it with coffee, taking the creamer out of the fridge and pouring some in. Chunks swirled at the top. I stood next to Mr. Kinson and waited to pour it out in the sink. He didn't smell like I'd expected, cologne or aftershave, like the musky-apple smelling stuff my father had always worn. This was something sweeter, like an off-brand laundry detergent.

"You drink coffee?" he asked, still scrubbing at his mug. There was a dark stain inside it that looked like the rings of a tree.

"Not today, I guess. The creamer's gone bad."

"Here." He leaned back so I could dump it over a dirty plate and knife. His hands were smooth and pink and there was hair on his knuckles. I noticed he wore a plain gold wedding ring.

"I didn't know you were married," I said. I let water fill up my Styrofoam cup, as if I were going to wash it and use it again.

"I don't talk about my personal life at group."

Close up, I could see the fuzzy hairs of his neck were more red than brown. His skin was steadily pinkening, the back of his ears darker than the rest of him.

"I'll see you next week, Julie." Opening the cabinet next to the fridge, he put in his mug without drying it, upside down. He left without looking at me.

Water dripped through the closed cabinet door. I opened it again and took out the mug, drying it with a wad of paper towels. The side of it said "Cici." I put it back in the cabinet and closed the door.

Draped in pearly white satin, I twirled in front of the mirror. I hadn't shaved my legs in a few weeks, but it didn't matter because the dress was long and fell all the way to the floor. The material was expensive and thick, but I'd had to forego my limp old bra because of its wide scoop neck. It was nicer than anything I'd ever owned. I dropped reams of platinum necklaces over my head, slipped a giant turquoise rock on my ring finger and scores of silver bangles on my wrists. Cecilia was still in her chenille robe. It was parted a little bit at her legs, a dark shadow cloaking whether she was wearing underwear.

"How do I look?" I leaned over the mannequin's shoulder to reach for a tube of peppermint-colored lipstick. It was waxy and slick, and it made me look like a little kid. I scrubbed it off with a tissue and put it back where I'd found it.

"My dad wouldn't let me wear make-up until I was in high school." I picked up a gold-backed hairbrush and ran it through my hair, which was already greasy at the roots though I'd washed it that morning. Cecilia's was thick and bountiful, almost too much for her own head. It made me want to snip some off for myself. "He said it was too old for me."

There were too many fragrances to choose from. I dabbed three separate scents on my wrists and neck, dotting a line between my breasts. The shoes were all size sixes, too small for my size-nine feet. I tried to put some on anyway, struggling on the ottoman, my armpits getting sweaty beneath the satin dress. I put them back on the rack and grabbed a bottle of nail polish instead, coating each toenail a brassy pink that made my toes look like Vienna sausages.

"Maybe you could help Cecilia dress." Mr. Kinson stood in the doorway, a dishtowel over his shoulder. He was smiling.

"Okay," I said, looking at the row of dresses. "I guess I could do that."

"Great. Dinner's in twenty."

During the day, I found myself compiling lists of things to do at night to keep me occupied: watch an entire season of a television show on Netflix, bake a layer cake from scratch using only ingredients we had in our ill-stocked kitchen, reorganize all of my books by genre and then alphabetically (title and then maybe by author). I taught myself to knit one night watching YouTube videos, perched in the weak light of my clip-on reading lamp. I made pot holders, the only shape that my fingers could articulate. I crafted dozens of things from life hack websites, including old CDs that I turned into Christmas ornaments and an iPhone speaker made out of a toilet paper roll.

Night was heavy as a wool blanket. It pressed in on all sides and made it hard to breathe. I'd never really spent time with any particular friends at school; there were a few girls I'd hung out with in marching band, but now I mostly spent time at home. David did the opposite. My brother was a year older than me and never around. When he finally stumbled home at night from basketball practice or dinners out with friends, he fell into bed and hibernated while I burned my retinas on the blue screen of the computer.

My bedroom was on the first floor of the house, far away from my brother and my mother upstairs. I prowled the crawl space for boxes of my old toys. It was only accessible through a hole in the ceiling of the hallway outside the living room. I stood on a chair and pushed up the painted plywood until it slid up and over. The crawl space was dark, but I used the flashlight on my phone to see the box just inside. It was labeled with block print, my name, Julie, and the word BARBIES.

It was hard to reach. In addition to the chair, I had to add the dictionary from the shelf in my father's den, which sat dark and lonely at the far end of the house. None of us went in there, except to get sheets of plain white paper from the printer. His computer desk sat covered with the minutia of his life: the last newspaper he'd read, an empty glass of orange juice spotted with fragments of dried pulp. Even climbing on top, I could just barely reach the box's cardboard lip. I jumped a little and felt the cover of the dictionary slide beneath my feet. As I pulled the box down, I slipped a little and felt the chair wobble up onto two legs beneath me, like a startled horse.

I took the box back into my room and sat it on the rug.

Pulling out the newspaper stuffed into the top, I was on the lookout for silverfish and roaches, but there were none, just the trace evidence that they'd once been there—brown droppings in the Barbies' long hair. I sat them in a pile; some of them unclothed, some of them in ball gowns and swimsuits, one in a pink plastic hula skirt that had deteriorated to the just a shiny elasticized belt. There were two lonely unclothed Kens. I left them sitting in the bottom of the box.

One Barbie was a Wizard of Oz replica: Glinda the Good Witch. I'd gotten her for Christmas when I was six. She wore a large pink dress and a crown, and her fairy wand had a star stuck at the end with glittery streamers. My father had gone out at the last minute to pick her up because he knew how much I loved the movie. Her face was perfectly sculpted with high cheekbones and curved lips. Her eyes were the largest portion of her face, twinkles drawn in with white paint to make her vision look perpetually starry.

Light creeped gray over the windowsill and I heard the sound of a bird trilling obnoxiously close to the house. I turned off the light to my room and the alarm on my phone, knowing that my mother wouldn't wake me.

Glinda lay beside me on the pillow. I traced her hair, which smelled like mildew and vinyl. I breathed her in and rested my lips against her face while the sun fell down on us from the window glass in warm squares of light.

It was easy to get the mannequin out of the robe, but much harder to get her into a dress. I picked through a few different gowns before settling on the blue velvet. It had some stretch and zipped up the back. "This is definitely your color." I waved it in front of her like a matador. "Look at those baby blues."

Her drink was dripping sweat. I loosened the velcro and set it on the counter before deciding I should just drink it myself. The ice had melted and the bourbon went down easier than the first. It gave everything a soft, fuzzy edge, like when my allergies kicked up and I took Benadryl.

"I have brown eyes. My dad used to sing that song to me, that old one? Don't you make my brown eyes blue, something like that, I think." I touched her hair, let my fingers tangle in its thickness. "The singer had really long hair that came down to the floor. I used to tell him I wanted a haircut like that."

She was wearing a lace demi bra and matching underwear beneath the robe. Through the thin knit, I could see she had pubic hair. The outline of her nipples stood out through the cloth. I worked the dress up her legs and kneeled on the ground at her feet, carefully pulling her up out of the seat and into my arms when the dress reached her waist. She was heavier than I'd anticipated, but not as much a real human body. It was manageable. Her weight rested solidly against me as I pulled up the dress and got it over both arms.

"My dad had brown eyes, too. Really happy squinty eyes, like he was always smiling, even when he wasn't." I slid the dress up and rested her back in the chair again. "That was a thing I used to always tell people about us, that we looked the same because we looked like we were always happy, even if we weren't."

Her hair was in her face. I pulled it back and French braided it, my fingers unused to that much hair. I had to do it more than once, just to make sure the loop of it didn't swerve to the right of her head. Tendrils fell out and danced along her cheeks. I smoothed them back, tucking them into the space on her wooden skull that was sculpted to look like ears.

"All set?" Mr. Kinson had changed into a nice button down shirt and khaki slacks. His hair was damp and brushed back off his forehead.

"Yeah, I think so."

"Two lovely ladies for dinner tonight! I'm so lucky."

Cecilia looked lighter than paper as he picked her up and carried her out.

There was a big bag of clay set up on the sideboard next to the sink, and there were a few pottery wheels placed around the room. A few of the other girls had gotten there early, too, and we all stood around digging our hands down into the slippery gray mixture.

"What the hell are we even going to do with this?" Lindsay picked up a big, slick ball of the stuff and crushed it between her fingers. Bits of it broke apart and fell onto the linoleum.

"I don't know, probably make a bowl or something." I smoothed the clay along my hand until the raised whirls of my fingerprint stood out like brands.

"This isn't even the art I do."

I looked at her. She had on a black t-shirt and ripped jeans. Her shoes were little canvas slips with holes bursting along either side. "What kind of art do you do?" I asked.

She looked at the blob in her hand; the sides of it indented by her fingers. She stuffed it back in the bag. "I sing, like in a show choir."

Mr. Kinson walked in from the back room. He was wearing a green smock over his white collared shirt and his hair was scrubbed back into a tiny ponytail; I thought he looked like an over-the-hill bag boy. "Go ahead and find a seat." He thunked another plastic bag of clay onto the counter top. "We'll do group share first, then we'll get to the project portion."

The chairs were pushed into a circle. I looked at Mr. Kinson and imagined him painting nude portraits of his mannequin alone in his art studio. I wondered if she had a body like my Barbies, all smooth without any indentations, not even a belly button, or if she was like one of those sex dolls with a crotch carved out for penetration.

Micah was a short kid with dark mustache and gelled hair. His mother had died of breast cancer two years ago; he talked in group about it almost weekly. He didn't seem to connect with the things he was saying about his mother—who he claimed cooked better than half the neighborhood and worked out to Jane Fonda aerobics tapes in the garage, even during her last few rounds of chemo.

"This is my mother's atlas," he said, opening to a middle section and holding it in front of him like a hymnal. In his small hands, the book looked humongous. "She loved to look at it while she sat at our kitchen table, picking out all the places she'd love to travel. She never got to go very far, but I knew she went there in her mind."

Micah pawed at the book like he was petting a cat. None us spoke of the dead like he did, like he was reciting lines from a play.

"Great, Micah. Really great." Mr. Kinson looked at me, then down at the floor. "Julie, you have something to share?"

A plastic grocery bag sat on the floor between my feet. I reached down into it and pulled out Barbie's pink convertible. "It's a T-top," I said, pointing to the pink plastic crossbar in the middle. It had seat belts that dangled loose out the windows. There was no Barbie inside it, but I had a few in the bag. "My dad gave it to me when I broke my arm."

"Why is this special to you?"

"It's not." I sat back down and looked at the grocery bag between my knees. A tiny hand poked through the top. Its fingers had been chewed on by our family cat, Czar Nicholas, back when I was in the second grade.

"Why not?"

"Because dolls are for kids, aren't they?" I asked, staring hard at Mr. Kinson. "We give them up when we get older."

After a pause, Mr. Kinson stood up. "That's enough circle for today," he said, gesturing at the wheels behind him. "Grab some clay. We're going to make mugs."

We drank red wine with dinner from crystal goblets. It was the most alcohol I'd ever consumed, excluding the summer between ninth and tenth grade when a few girls at band camp bought wine coolers for our bunk. We drank them all and went swimming in the lake behind the cabins. I remember feeling a lot like I did now; like I was floating, that there was nothing holding my body to the planet.

I dripped some wine on the tabletop as I reached for more bread. "I'm sorry," I said, dabbing at it with some water. "This is all really good."

"Wait until you see dessert." Mr. Kinson smiled and fed Cecilia another bite. The noodles hung limp from the fork. Her mouth a perpetually parted smile. "Chocolate lava cake."

"Do you usually cook like this for guests?"

"We don't usually have guests, Julie."

Light flickered on the table from strategically placed silver candlesticks. The tablecloth was thick and white, like the kind they used at nice restaurants. I worried that I would spill some of the wine on my dress, and then I stopped worrying altogether and just let my mind swim free. Mr. Kinson had set my Barbie up on the tabletop beside my plate. She was still wearing her pink dress, but it looked orange in the light. Her face was similar to Cecilia's; they both had high cheekbones and big eyes. I drank more wine and was surprised when I finished the glass. Mr. Kinson poured more and pushed it into my hand.

"If you two are done, why don't you retire to the dressing room while I fix the dessert and clean everything up?"

There were two group members to every pottery wheel. I let my clay flop wildly on the stand and barely touched it as it spun. It refused to remain upright, collapsing into what resembled a melting flowerpot, aggressively ugly and pitted by the scrape of my fingernails. When I finally got the middle to indent into a semblance of a cup, I turned off the wheel and got up to let Lindsay have her turn.

"This is stupid," she said. "What does any of this have to do with therapy?" She had clay streaked on her chin from where she'd tried to wipe at her lipstick. It looked a little like a goatee.

"Do you really want to talk about your sister right now?" I took a surplus piece of clay and fashioned a crude handle that I attached to the side of what barely resembled a mug.

There were a couple of cardboard boxes on the table at the side of the room. I stuck my creation inside one and went to wash my hands. When I came back, Mr. Kinson was etching my initials into the lopsided bottom of the mug.

"I don't want my name on that," I said, taking it from him and putting it back into the box. There were already five other clay structures inside, most just as mangled as mine. Micah dropped his in last; he'd carved his mother's name into the side with a heart around it.

"I'll take this home and fire them in my kiln," Mr. Kinson said, patting the side of the box. "We can glaze them next week."

As people left, I stalled and looked at my phone. I was supposed to call my mother when we were through, but she'd had a bad week and would be in bed, and I didn't feel right calling her. David had a basketball game out of town and was spending the night somewhere, again, for the third night in a row.

"Julie, could you help me carry these to my van?" Mr. Kinson held one of the open cardboard boxes. The other sat on the counter top. I went and picked up the second, walking carefully behind him, making sure I held the box straight up so that the mugs wouldn't fall sideways and crush each other. My plastic grocery bag dug into my arm from where I'd looped it; the Barbies inside poked hard against my stomach.

The parking lot was nearly empty. Lindsay was climbing into her car; she waved at me over her steering wheel as she pulled out of the parking lot. Stooping down at the back of the van, Mr. Kinson set down the box carefully and opened the door with his key. I waited, wondering what I'd see beneath the blankets: the huddled shape of a corpse, maybe a bare leg poking out from under the sheets. But there was nothing—not even a pillow. There was just clean gray carpet.

"Just set them down here." He put his box down at the back of the van. "They should be pretty solid."

"Okay." I put mine down next to his, until the sides were lined up and snug. When I moved the grocery bag off my arm, there was a red indentation from where the loops had dug into my skin.

"Can I see those?"

"What?"

"The Barbies," he said, reaching over and gently taking the bag from my hand. He dug below the pink plastic convertible and pulled out Glinda. Her crown had gone askew and sat pressed down over the right side of her face. He softly finger-combed her hair. Overhead a plane flew past. It was quiet enough I could hear the sound of my breathing and the traffic far off down the street.

"It's a very nice doll." The back of his van smelled faintly of chemicals and cleaners. "Probably pretty expensive. Your father got this for you?"

"Yes."

"He must have loved you very much to do that."

"Maybe. I don't think spending money means much. I don't know anything about him, who he was. I thought I knew things, but it turns out none of it was true." I shrugged and looked down at my feet. One of my shoelaces was untied and dragging in some chewing gum. "How much can you know about any person, though, really?"

Mr. Kinson smiled. His teeth were a little brown at the root and his gums were pink, but his breath smelled like spearmint. "That's very true." His thumb rubbed against the doll's hair, smoothing it. "My wife really loves dolls, too."

"That's cool, I guess."

"Would you like to meet her?" He said this staring at a space over my shoulder, back toward the building. "You could have dinner with us, if you're not too busy."

I still hadn't called my mother. Sometimes our meetings went long, and I was sure she was still lying in bed, on her side, the left side, my father's pillow plumped up beside her and one of his white undershirts tucked up beneath her chin.

"Okay."

He smiled again and closed the trunk. Walking around the side of the van closest to the shade tree, he opened the driver's side door. I stared at the passenger seat. There sat the mannequin, dressed in white tennis shorts and a knit halter top with red and blue stripes. There were pristine sneakers on her feet and she had a terrycloth sweatband around her wooden forehead. On her lap was a brand new tennis racquet.

"Julie, I'd like you to meet my wife. Cecilia."

Her eyes were deep and large, taking up most of her face. She sat smiling, quietly, facing front. One of her hands held a tennis ball. It was velcroed to her wrist.

Everything smelled like chocolate. I'd gotten Cecilia back down the hall and into her dressing room, carefully maneuvering and avoiding doorways and furniture. Music still piped through the speakers, now soft jazz, the kind my mother liked to listen to when she cleaned the house.

The mannequin smelled good, like powdered sugar and cookies. I took off her dress and put her robe back on, slipping her wooden feet into a pair of fluffy pink slippers. Glinda sat on the vanity. I stuck a marabou scarf around her body, and then looped one around my own neck until I felt like I couldn't breathe and took it off again.

There was a plush golden footstool near Cecilia's chair. I pulled it up beside her and looked at both of our reflections. Hers was wise and kind, her twinkling eyes seemed to say:

You can tell me anything, Julie.

"I know that," I said, putting my hand on hers. "I know I can tell you anything."

I leaned closer to her until our noses touched. Up close, I could see the tiny cracks that ran through the paint on her face. Her eyes merged into one blue Cyclops orb that fuzzed and radiated outward until it made me dizzy.

You seem stressed.

"I am. I really am." Eskimo kisses with a mannequin were strange; her nose had no give. "Can I tell you something, Cecilia? A secret?"

Of course you can. I'm a really good listener.

I closed my eyes and pressed my lips to hers. They were smooth and cool. "My father wasn't actually very nice," I whispered, leaning close to her ear, beneath the swoop of her dark hair. "He used to hit my mom sometimes, when he was drinking. And he'd tell David that he was stupid and that sports were pointless." I laid my head on Cecilia's shoulder, breathing in her powder scent and letting the fuzz wash over me. "One time I accidentally burned a pot of macaroni and cheese. He told me that I'd make a terrible mother. He took away all my dolls and put them in the crawlspace."

I'm sorry, Julie.

Snuggling into her neck, I smoothed my hands up and down the thick satin of my dress and let myself feel floaty and good. I looked at our twin reflections again, beautiful sisters, and noticed a bright red dot hovering between our faces. Squinting, I leaned forward and pressed my finger to the dot. When I turned around, I could see it coming from between the racks of clothes on the wall directly behind us. Padding over, I pulled the dresses apart on either side and saw a wooden cabinet lodged in the wall. When I pulled open the doors, there was a small silver camera inside. The light radiated from the front where it glowed red over the record button.

Legs folded beneath me, I sat in the back of the van with the uncooked mugs and let my body rock back and forth as Mr. Kinson drove. His neighborhood wasn't too far away from my own. I recognized the bare steeple of the Methodist church as we rounded a corner, and there was the intersection with the three gas stations near my school. I leaned into the curves, watching the wispy clouds float past. The branches of the trees stretched overhead through the dark snakes of telephone wires. The mannequin's hand was close to the window, and occasionally tapped the glass as we took curves and stopped at traffic lights

As he pulled into the driveway, her head suddenly lolled sideways. Her wooden forehead pressed against the window glass like a normal woman's might. She looked pensive, like she wasn't sure if she wanted to be home.

"Cecilia's got a bit of a neck problem." Mr Kinson reached over and righted her face until all I could see was the dark, shiny cloud of her hair. "I keep meaning to get it fixed, but I just can't part with her for even one night."

"Missing people is hard," I replied. The floor of the van was so clean. My mother's car was full of lint and dirt, little crunched up leaves dragged in by the bottoms of sneakers and paper take out bags and chewing gum wrappers.

"I'll come around."

"Okay."

The hatch lifted up and the sun streamed in behind his body, turning him into a dark silhouette. He put out a hand and pulled me forward, until I sat with my legs dangling out the end.

"Grab your box, we'll put these directly in the kiln."

I followed him around the side of the house, a one-story ranch the color of slate. The shutters at the side of each window were painted a lacquered black. Every pane had vertical blinds. At the back was an open fence that led into the yard. Round concrete stepping stones led to a building the size of a shed. Mr. Kinson used a key to unlock the padlock and flipped on the light. There was an easel and paints and a table in the center with more bags of clay and a stained batch of aprons. In the far corner, against the wall, was a round metal canister on three squat legs.

Setting his box on the table, he began pulling the mugs out and placing them in rows. I set my box down beside his and did the same.

"So you sculpt?" I asked, deliberately digging my fingernails into Micah's mug until the handle broke off.

"My wife did. Does." He stopped for a second and then wiped his hand along his brow. The room was very warm and the kiln wasn't even on yet. Mr. Kinson placed all the clay pieces inside and then showed me how to work the controls. "Once you lock the lid, it's on—you can't open it again until the firing is complete. We won't turn it on yet; we can't leave it alone while it works. After dinner."

Her head detached easily. It weighed about as much as a bowling ball, maybe less. I carried it under my arm, still gowned in the white satin dress. Her hair draped down my waist and swung against me with every step.

"I'm going to use the bathroom, okay?' I called down the hall, toward the direction of the kitchen.

"Okay! I'm plating the dessert."

"Could I have some more wine?"

"Sure! I'll open another bottle."

A door connected the dressing room to a large, opulent bathroom tiled in white and black Carrera marble. A huge claw foot tub took up one corner of the room and there was a shower with multiple heads beside a large window.

I'd taken the camcorder and the stack of tapes in the cabinet. Unlatching the window, I opened it wide and threw out the head and the electronics, then climbed over the sill holding my plastic grocery bag. I'd stuffed my own clothes inside with my Barbies and the pink convertible.

The grass was dewy and I wasn't wearing shoes. I walked carefully across the yard, avoiding acorns and sharp bits of stick. The shed was still unlocked. I walked inside and flipped on the overhead light, setting the head and the camera and the tapes down on the table as I readied the kiln for firing.

First went the camcorder and the tapes, all labeled with different names: FLEUR and BELLA and STEPHIE and MELISSA. Mine was still in the camera. There was no name attached yet. I pulled off the dress and threw it in, putting on my dirty jeans and bra and t-shirt with the hole in the armpit. Everything smelled like home.

On top of everything went the head. A few of the mugs squashed flat beneath the weight. Cecilia looked out at me with her wide, unblinking eyes. I smoothed down her hair and patted her lips. I pulled Glinda from my plastic bag and set her down beside Cecilia. Closing the lid, I selected the highest temperature and locked the kiln.

DEFINING HURRICANE

DERRICK AUSTIN

Water's unrelief, a backhand
from miles away; sidewalks
overcome and newly green;

the backwash of gutters;
welcome mats both taunt
and entreaty; signs bent

as if in prayer; the military mobilizes,
or not; those who return count
the missing like worry beads—

water-warped buildings
under a bleached sky
where we rebuild and wait.

ABOUT THE CONTRIBUTORS

KRISTEN ARNETT is a fiction and essay writer who has held fellowships at *Kenyon Review, Tin House,* and *Lambda Literary Foundation.* She was awarded *Ninth Letter*'s 2015 Literary Award in Fiction, was runner-up for the 2016 Robert Watson Literary Prize at *The Greensboro Review,* and was a finalist for *Indiana Review's* 2016 Fiction Prize. Her work has appeared or is upcoming at *North American Review, The Normal School, Volume 1 Brooklyn,* OSU's *The Journal, Catapult, Bennington Review, Portland Review, Tin House* Flash Fridays/*The Guardian, Salon, The Rumpus*, and elsewhere. Her debut story collection, *Felt in the Jaw*, will be published by Split Lip Press in 2017. She is represented by Pande Literary Agency.

DERRICK AUSTIN is the author of *Trouble the Water* (BOA Editions). A Cave Canem fellow, his work has appeared in *Best American Poetry 2015*, *Image: A Journal of Arts and Religion, New England Review, Nimrod,* and other anthologies and publications. He was a finalist for the 2017 Kate Tufts Discovery Award.

JOHN BRANDON has published three novels and a story collection, all with McSweeney's Press. He was born and raised on the Gulf Coast of Florida, but now lives in Minnesota, where he teaches at Hamline University. He has spent time as the Grisham Fellow at Ole Miss and as the Tickner Fellow at Gilman School.

NATHAN DEUEL is the author of *Friday Was the Bomb: Five Years in the Middle East,* an Amazon Best Book of the Month. He has written essays, reviews, and short fiction for *The New York Times Magazine, Harper's, GQ,* and *The Paris Review,* among others. He lives in Los Angeles and teaches undergraduate writing at UCLA Writing Programs and graduate writing at the MFA in Creative Writing at Mount Saint Mary's University.

JAQUIRA DÍAZ is the 2016-18 *Kenyon Review* Fellow in Prose and recipient of two Pushcart Prizes, an Elizabeth George Foundation Grant, the Carl Djerassi Fiction Fellowship from the Wisconsin Institute for Creative Writing, and an NEA Fellowship to the Hambidge Center for the Arts. She's been awarded fellowships from The MacDowell Colony, the Virginia Center for the Creative Arts, the Ragdale Foundation, and elsewhere. Her work has appeared in *The Best American Essays 2016*, *Rolling Stone*, *The Guardian*, *The FADER*, *The Sun*, the *Kenyon Review*, *Brevity*, and elsewhere. She was born in Puerto Rico and grew up in Miami Beach.

ASHA DORE'S essays and stories have recently appeared in *The Rumpus*, *theNewerYork*, *Treehouse*, *Best of the Net*, and other venues. She lives in Oregon with her husband, two amazing daughters, and a herd of invisible horses who sleep in the guest bathroom and are not to be disturbed.

JOHN HENRY FLEMING is the author of *Songs for the Deaf*, *The Legend of the Barefoot Mailman*, *Fearsome Creatures of Florida*, and *The Book I Will Write*. Lately he's been writing Executive Branch lyrics at songofhimself.com. He teaches in the MFA program at the University of South Florida, where he's the founder and advisory editor of *Saw Palm: Florida Literature and Art*. His website is johnhenryfleming.com.

SOHRAB HOMI FRACIS was the first Asian to win the Iowa Short Fiction Award, juried by the Iowa Writers Workshop, for his first book, *Ticket to Minto: Stories of India and America*. It was also published in India and Germany. He has an M.A. in English / Creative Writing from University of North Florida, where he later taught literature and creative writing. He is on the Critique Sessions faculty at Florida Heritage Book Festival. He was Visiting Writer in Residence at Augsburg College and twice Artist in Residence at Yaddo. He has received the Florida Individual Artist Fellowship in Literature, the Walter E. Dakin Fellowship in Fiction, and now in 2017, on the heels of his timely new novel *Go Home*, the SALA (South Asian Literary Association) Distinguished Achievement Award for Creative Writing.

SARAH GERARD is the author of the novel *Binary Star* (Two Dollar Radio), the essay collection *Sunshine State* (Harper Perennial), and two chapbooks, most recently *BFF* (Guillotine). Her short stories, essays, interviews, and criticism have appeared in *The New York Times*, *Granta*, *New York Magazine*'s "The Cut," *The Paris Review Daily*, *The Los Angeles Review of Books*, *Bookforum*, *Joyland*, *Vice*, *BOMB Magazine*, and other journals, as well as anthologies. She's been supported by fellowships and residencies from Yaddo, Tin House, and PlatteForum. She writes a monthly column on food for *Hazlitt* and teaches writing in New York City.

RACQUEL HENRY is a Trinidadian writer and editor with an MFA from Fairleigh Dickinson University. She is also a part-time English Professor and owns the writing center, Writer's Atelier, in Winter Park, FL. In 2010 Racquel co-founded *Black Fox Literary Magazine* where she still serves as an editor. She is also a board member for The Jack Kerouac Project, an Orlando-based writing residency. Her fiction, poetry, and nonfiction have appeared in places like *The Rusty Nail, Lotus-Eater Magazine, The Best of There Will Be Words 2014 Chapbook, La Mensajera, Moko Caribbean Arts & Letters,* and *Reaching Beyond the Saguaros: A Collaborative Prosimetric Travelogue* (Serving House Books, 2017), among others.

SHANE HINTON is the author the story collection *Pinkies*. He teaches writing at the University of Tampa and lives in the winter strawberry capital of the world.

LINDSAY HUNTER is the author of the novels *Eat Only When You're Hungry* and *Ugly Girls,* and the story collections *Don't Kiss Me* and *Daddy's*. She lives in Chicago with her husband, sons, and dogs.

KEVIN MOFFETT is the author of two story collections and a collaborative novel, *The Silent History*. His stories and essays have appeared in *McSweeney's, Tin House, American Short Fiction, The Believer, The Best American Short Stories* and elsewhere. He has received the National Magazine Award, the Nelson Algren Award, the Pushcart Prize and a literature fellowship from the National Endowment of the Arts. He teaches at Claremont McKenna College and in the low-residency MFA at the University of Tampa.

ALISSA NUTTING is author of the novels *Tampa* and *Made for Love,* and the short-story collection *Unclean Jobs for Women and Girls*. She is an assistant professor of English and creative writing at Grinnell College in Iowa.

JASON OCKERT is the author of *Wasp Box,* a novel, and two collections of short stories: *Neighbors of Nothing* and *Rabbit Punches*. Winner of the Dzanc Short Story Collection Contest, the Atlantic Monthly Fiction Contest, and the Mary Roberts Rinehart Award, he was also a finalist for the Shirley Jackson Award and the Million Writers Award. His work has appeared in journals and anthologies including *Best American Mystery Stories, Oxford American, One Story,* and *McSweeney's*.

AMY PARKER is a Tampa Bay area native, but she's an MFA in Creative Writing student at Eastern Oregon University's low-residency program. She specializes in creative nonfiction. Her work has appeared in *Oregon East* and *Punchnel's*.

JEFF PARKER has written several books, including the nonfiction book *Where Bears Roam the Streets: A Russian Journal* (Harper Collins), the novel *Ovenman* (Tin House), and the story collection *The Taste of Penny* (Dzanc). His fiction and nonfiction have appeared in the *Best American Nonrequired Reading*, *Ploughshares*, *Tin House*, *The Walrus*, and many others. With Pasha Malla, he co-"wrote" the collection of found sports poetry *Erratic Fire, Erratic Passion* (Featherproof), and with Annie Liontas he edited *A Manner of Being* (University of Massachusetts Press), a book of essays by writers on their mentors. With Mikhail Iossel he edited two collections of writing by contemporary Russian writers, *Rasskazy: New Fiction from a New Russia* (Tin House) and *Amerika: Russian Writers View the United States* (Dalkey Archive). With Alina Ryabovolova and Mariya Gusev he translated the novel *Sankya* by Zakhar Prilepin from the Russian. He is the Director and co-founder of the DISQUIET International Literary Program in Lisbon, Portugal, and he teaches in the MFA program at the University of Massachusetts Amherst.

MICHAEL J. SEIDLINGER is an Asian American author of a number of novels including *My Pet Serial Killer*, *The Fun We've Had* and *The Strangest*. He serves as director of publicity at Dzanc Books, book reviews editor at Electric Literature, and publisher in chief of Civil Coping Mechanisms, an indie press specializing in innovative fiction, nonfiction, and poetry. He lives in Brooklyn, New York, where he never sleeps and is forever searching for the next best cup of coffee. You can find him online at michaeljseidlinger.com, on Facebook, and on Twitter (@mjseidlinger).

LAURA VAN DEN BERG was raised in Florida and earned her M.F.A. at Emerson College. Her first novel, *Find Me*, published by FSG in 2015, was selected as a "Best Book of 2015" by NPR, *Time Out New York*, and *BuzzFeed*, among others, in addition to being longlisted for the 2016 International Dylan Thomas Prize. She is also the author of two collections of stories, *What the World Will Look Like When All the Water Leaves Us* (Dzanc Books, 2009) and *The Isle of Youth* (FSG, 2013). *What the World* was a Barnes & Noble

"Discover Great New Writers" selection and shortlisted for the Frank O'Connor International Short Story Award. *The Isle of Youth* was named a "Best Book of 2013" by over a dozen outlets, including NPR, *The Boston Globe*, and *O, The Oprah Magazine*; a finalist for the Frank O'Connor Award; and received The Rosenthal Family Foundation Award from the American Academy of Arts & Letters and the 2015 Bard Fiction Prize. Her stories have appeared in *Conjunctions*, *Freeman's*, *The Kenyon Review*, *American Short Fiction*, *Ploughshares*, *Glimmer Train*, *One Story*, and have been anthologized in The Best American Short Stories, The Best American Mystery Stories, The O. Henry Prize Stories, The Best American Nonrequired Reading, and the Pushcart Prize XXIV. Her reviews and essays have appeared in *The New York Times Book Review*, *O, The Oprah Magazine*, and Vogue.com.

LIDIA YUKNAVITCH is the author of *The Book of Joan*; the National Bestselling novel *The Small Backs of Children*, winner of the 2016 Oregon Book Award's Ken Kesey Award for Fiction as well as the Reader's Choice Award; the novel *Dora: A Headcase*; as well as three books of short fictions – *Her Other Mouths*, *Liberty's Excess*, and *Real TO Reel*, and a critical book on war and narrative, *Allegories Of Violence* (Routledge). Her widely acclaimed memoir *The Chronology of Water* was a finalist for a PEN Center USA award for creative nonfiction and winner of a PNBA Award and the Oregon Book Award Reader's Choice. *The Misfit's Manifesto*, a book based on her recent TED Talk, is forthcoming. She has also had writing appear in publications including *Guernica Magazine*, *Ms.*, *The Iowa Review*, *Zyzzyva*, *Another Chicago Magazine*, *The Sun*, *Exquisite Corpse*, *TANK*, and in the anthologies *Life As We Show It* (City Lights), *Wreckage of Reason* (Spuytin Duyvil), *Forms at War* (FC2), *Feminaissance* (Les Figues Press), and *Representing Bisexualities* (SUNY), as well as online at *The Rumpus*. She founded the workshop series Corporeal Writing in Portland Oregon, where she teaches both in person and online. She received her doctorate in Literature from the University of Oregon. She lives in Oregon with her husband Andy Mingo and their renaissance man son, Miles. She is a very good swimmer.

MORE FROM FLORIDA...

FANTASTIC FLORIDAS

Burrow Press' weekly online journal featuring new fiction, essays, poetry, interviews, excerpts, art, et cetera.

BURROWPRESS.COM/FLORIDA

SUBSCRIBE

Burrow publishes four, carefully selected books each year, offered in an annual subscription package for a mere $60 (which is like $5/month, $0.20/day, or 1 night at the bar). Subscribers directly contribute to helping us build a lasting body of literature and fostering literary community in Orlando and Florida. Since 2010 we've provided over 800 opportunities for writers to publish and share their work, but we can't keep doing it without your help. We survive on subscriptions, learn more at:

BURROWPRESS.COM/SUBSCRIBE

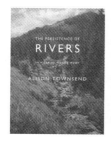  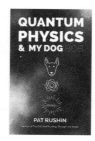 

the illiterati

2017 SUBSCRIBERS

ORLANDOANS
Secret Society Goods
Stephanie Rizzo
Dustin Bowersett
Hunter Choate
Patrick Rushin
Stacy Barton
Marcella Benton
Roberta Alfonso Malone
Catherine Carson
Lora Waring
Naomi Butterfield
Nayma Russi
Nathan Holic

SUBSCRIBERS
Mike Wheaton
Mary Nesler
Emily Dziuban
Dowell Bethea
Sarah Wildeman
Ginger Duggan
Ashley French
Spencer Rhodes
Lauren Groff
Susan Fallows
Sean Walsh
Liesl Swogger
Shawn McKee
Shane Hinton

Janna Benge
Stacey Matrazzo
John Upperco
Peter Bacopoulos
Mike Cabrera
Sara Isaac
Kevin Craig
Stephen Cagnina
Lisa Roney
Joyce Sharman
Amy Parker
Martha Brenckle
Thomas M. Bunting Projects
Denise Gottshalk
Jessica Penza
Sarah Curley
Mike Cuglietta
Jonathan Kosik
H Blaine Strickland
Pat Green
Sarah Taitt
Winston Taitt
Susan Frith
Benjamin Noel
Matthew Lang
David Poissant
Erin Hartigan
Isabel Arias
Erika Friedlander
Amy Sindler

the illiterati

2017 SUBSCRIBERS

Kirsten Holz
Dan Reiter
Alexander Lenhoff
Rebecca Fortes
Giti Khalsa
Nikki Barnes
Jeremy Bassetti
Mira Tanna
Rita Barnes
Chuck Dinkins
Stuart Buchanan
Rich Wahl
Tyler Koon
Bob Lipscomb
Christie Hill
Craig Ustler
Lauren Zimmerman
Laura Albert
Emily Willix
Danielle Kessinger
Elisabeth Dang
Vicki Nelson
Camile Araujo
Leslie Salas
Cindy Simmons
Lauren Mitchell
Peter Knocke
Teresa Carmody
Lauren Georgia
Susan Lilley

Jeffrey Shuster
Susan Pascalar
Michael Gualandri
Jessica Horton
Jason Katz

LOCALS
Kim Robinson
Delila Smalley
Christine Daniel
Karen Rigsby
Tod Caviness
Terri Ackley
Terry Thaxton
Danita Berg
Karen Roby
Jesse Bradley
JT Taylor
Ben Comer
Grace Fiandaca
Aaron Harriss
Jonathan Miller
Pamela Gilbert
Yana Keyzerman
Nylda Dieppa-Aldarondo
Leeann M. Lee
Gerry Wolfson-Grande

MORE FROM BURROW PRESS

PINKIES: STORIES
by Shane Hinton

Absurdist short stories about fatherhood.

"If Kafka got it on with Flannery O' Connor, *Pinkies* would be their love child."

–Lidia Yuknavitch, author of *The Book of Joan*

SONGS FOR THE DEAF: STORIES
by John Henry Fleming

Modern spins on the American tall tale.

"A joyful, deranged, endlessly surprising book of stories that defy easy categorization. Fleming's prose is glorious music; his rhythms will get into your bloodstream, and his images will sink into your dreams."

–Karen Russell, *Swamplandia!*

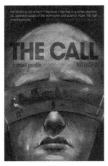

THE CALL: A VIRTUAL PARABLE
by Pat Rushin

Like *Waiting for Godot* with high-speed internet access.

"Pat Rushin is out of his fucking mind. I like that in a writer; that and his daredevil usage of the semi-colon and asterisk make *The Call* unputdownable."

–Terry Gilliam, director of *Brazil*

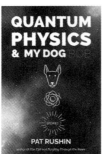

QUANTUM PHYSICS & MY DOG BOB: STORIES
by Pat Rushin

Quirky stories that fuse the familiar and the uncanny.

"Brilliant and funny, these stories will easily change the way you observe the world."

–Virgil Suarez, author of *The Soviet Circus Comes to Havana*

15 VIEWS OF MIAMI
edited by Jaquira Díaz

Named one of the 7 best books about Miami by the Miami New Times and one of "our ten favorite books set in South Florida" by The New Tropic.

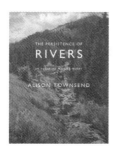

THE PERSISTENCE OF RIVERS:
AN ESSAY ON MOVING WATER
by Alison Townsend

Evoking Thoreau and Dillard, a meditation on a life lived near rivers.

"A lyrical stream of relationships, reflections, and healing, crafted as smooth as the gurgling brooks and rivers intertwined in this wonderful collection of short essays."

–Todd Miller, Arcadia Books

TRAIN SHOTS: STORIES
by Vanessa Blakeslee

Pop stars, junkie doctors, train conductors. All depressed.

"*Train Shots* is more than a promising first collection by a formidably talented writer; it is a haunting story collection of the first order. I was flat knocked out. Blakeslee's range and confidence are astonishing."

–John Dufresne, *No Regrets, Coyote*

FORTY MARTYRS
by Philip F. Deaver

An ode to small towns and Midwestern lives.

"I could hardly stop reading, from first to last."

–Ann Beattie, *The State We're In*